THE DEW BREAKER

THE DEW BREAKER

Edwidge Danticat

ALFRED A. KNOPF  NEW YORK 2004

This Is a Borzoi Book Published by Alfred A. Knopf
Copyright © 2004 by Edwidge Danticat

All rights reserved under International and Pan-American Copyright Conventions
Published in the United States by Alfred A. Knopf, a division of Random House, Inc.,
New York, and simultaneously in Canada by Random House of Canada, Limited,
Toronto. Distributed by Random House, Inc., New York.
www.aaknopf.com

"The Book of the Dead," "Seven," and "Water Child" first appeared in *The New Yorker.*
"Seven" also appeared in *Best American Short Stories 2002* (Houghton Mifflin, 2002) and
The O'Henry Prize Stories 2002 (Doubleday, 2002). "The Book of Miracles" first appeared
in slightly different form as "The Dew Breaker" in *Gumbo: A Literary Rent Party*
(Broadway Books, 2002). "Night Talkers" appeared in *Callaloo* (Fall 2002) and in
Best American Short Stories 2003 (Houghton Mifflin, 2003). An earlier version of
"Monkey Tails" appeared as "From the Journals of Water Days 1986" in *Callaloo*
in 1989 and again in *Making Callaloo: 25 Years of Black Literature* (St. Martin's
Press, 2002). An earlier, and much shorter, version of "The Dew Breaker"
appeared as "Dies Irae" in *Conjunctions* in 2000.

Library of Congress Cataloging-in-Publication Data
Danticat, Edwidge, [date]
The dew breaker / Edwidge Danticat.— 1st ed.
p.   cm.
ISBN 1-4000-4114-7 (alk. paper)
1. Haiti—Fiction.   2. Haitian Americans—Fiction.   3. Brooklyn
(New York, N.Y.)—Fiction.   4. Torture—Fiction.   I. Title.
PS3554.A5815O86 2004
813'.54—dc22   2003060788

Manufactured in the United States of America
Published March 15, 2004
Reprinted Twice
Fourth Printing, May 2004

Maybe this is the beginning of madness . . .
Forgive me for what I am saying.
Read it . . . quietly, quietly.

—OSIP MANDELSTAM

CONTENTS

THE DEW BREAKER

THE BOOK OF THE DEAD

My father is gone. I'm slouched in a cast-aluminum chair across from two men, one the manager of the hotel where we're staying and the other a policeman. They're both waiting for me to explain what's become of him, my father.

The hotel manager—MR. FLAVIO SALINAS, the plaque on his office door reads—has the most striking pair of chartreuse eyes I've ever seen on a man with an island Spanish lilt to his voice.

The police officer, Officer Bo, is a baby-faced, short, white Floridian with a potbelly.

"Where are you and your daddy from, Ms. Bienaimé?" Officer Bo asks, doing the best he can with my last name. He does such a lousy job that, even though he and I and Salinas are the only people in Salinas' office, at first I think he's talking to someone else.

I was born and raised in East Flatbush, Brooklyn, and

have never even been to my parents' birthplace. Still, I answer "Haiti" because it is one more thing I've always longed to have in common with my parents.

Officer Bo plows forward with, "You all the way down here in Lakeland from Haiti?"

"We live in New York," I say. "We were on our way to Tampa."

"To do what?" Officer Bo continues. "Visit?"

"To deliver a sculpture," I say. "I'm an artist, a sculptor."

I'm really not an artist, not in the way I'd like to be. I'm more of an obsessive wood-carver with a single subject thus far—my father.

My creative eye finds Manager Salinas' office gaudy. The walls are covered with orange-and-green wallpaper, briefly interrupted by a giant gold leaf–bordered print of a Victorian cottage that resembles the building we're in.

Patting his light green tie, which brings out even more the hallucinatory shade of his eyes, Manager Salinas reassuringly tells me, "Officer Bo and I will do our best."

We start out with a brief description of my father: "Sixty-five, five feet eight inches, one hundred and eighty pounds, with a widow's peak, thinning salt-and-pepper hair, and velvet-brown eyes—"

"Velvet?" Officer Bo interrupts.

"Deep brown, same color as his complexion," I explain.

My father has had partial frontal dentures since he fell off his and my mother's bed and landed on his face ten years ago when he was having one of his prison nightmares. I mention that too. Just the dentures, not the nightmares. I also bring up the blunt, ropelike scar that runs from my father's right cheek down to the corner of his mouth, the only visible reminder of the year he spent in prison in Haiti.

"Please don't be offended by what I'm about to ask," Officer Bo says. "I deal with an older population here, and this is something that comes up a lot when they go missing. Does your daddy have any kind of mental illness, senility?"

I reply, "No, he's not senile."

"You have any pictures of your daddy?" Officer Bo asks.

My father has never liked having his picture taken. We have only a few of him at home, some awkward shots at my different school graduations, with him standing between my mother and me, his hand covering his scar. I had hoped to take some pictures of him on this trip, but he hadn't let me. At one of the rest stops I bought a disposable camera and pointed it at him anyway. As usual, he protested, covering his face with both hands like a little boy protecting his cheeks from a slap. He didn't want any more pictures taken of him for the rest of his life, he said, he was feeling too ugly.

"That's too bad," Officer Bo offers at the end of my too lengthy explanation. "He speaks English, your daddy? Can he ask for directions, et cetera?"

"Yes," I say.

"Is there anything that might make your father run away from you, particularly here in Lakeland?" Manager Salinas asks. "Did you two have a fight?"

I had never tried to tell my father's story in words before now, but my first completed sculpture of him was the reason for our trip: a three-foot mahogany figure of my father naked, kneeling on a half-foot-square base, his back arched like the curve of a crescent moon, his downcast eyes fixed on his very long fingers and the large palms of his hands. It was hardly revolutionary, rough and not too detailed, minimalist at best, but it was my favorite of all my attempted representations of my father. It was the way I had imagined him in prison.

The last time I had seen my father? The previous night, before falling asleep. When we pulled our rental car into the hotel's hedge-bordered parking lot, it was almost midnight. All the restaurants in the area were closed. There was nothing to do but shower and go to bed.

"It's like paradise here," my father had said when he'd seen our tiny room. It had the same orange-and-green wallpaper as Salinas' office, and the plush emerald carpet matched the walls. "Look, Ka," he said, his deep, raspy voice muted with exhaustion, "the carpet is like grass under our feet."

He'd picked the bed closest to the bathroom, removed the top of his gray jogging suit, and unpacked his toiletries. Soon after, I heard him humming loudly, as he always did, in the shower.

I checked on the sculpture, just felt it a little bit through the bubble padding and carton wrapping to make sure it was still whole. I'd used a piece of mahogany that was naturally flawed, with a few superficial cracks along what was now the back. I'd thought these cracks beautiful and had made no effort to sand or polish them away, as they seemed like the wood's own scars, like the one my father had on his face. But I was also a little worried about the cracks. Would they seem amateurish and unintentional, like a mistake? Could the wood come apart with simple movements or with age? Would the client be satisfied?

I closed my eyes and tried to picture the client to whom I was delivering the sculpture: Gabrielle Fonteneau, a Haitian American woman about my age, the star of a popular television series and an avid art collector. My friend Céline Benoit, a former colleague at the junior high school where I'm a substitute art teacher, had grown up with Gabrielle Fonteneau in Tampa and, at my request, on a holiday visit home had shown Gabrielle Fonteneau a snapshot of my *Father* piece and had persuaded her to buy it.

Gabrielle Fonteneau was spending the week away from Hollywood at her parents' house in Tampa. I took some time off, and both my mother and I figured that my father, who watched a lot of television, both at home and at his Nostrand Avenue barbershop, would enjoy meeting Gabrielle Fonteneau too. But when I woke up, my father was gone and so was the sculpture.

I stepped out of the room and onto the balcony overlooking the parking lot. It was a hot and muggy morning, the humid air laden with the smell of the freshly mowed tropical grass and sprinkler-showered hibiscus bordering the parking lot. My rental car too was gone. I hoped my father was driving around trying to find us some breakfast and would explain when he got back why he'd taken the sculpture with him, so I got dressed and waited. I watched a half hour of local morning news, smoked five mentholated cigarettes even though we were in a nonsmoking room, and waited some more.

All that waiting took two hours, and I felt guilty for having held back so long before going to the front desk to ask, "Have you seen my father?"

I feel Officer Bo's fingers gently stroking my wrist, perhaps to tell me to stop talking. Up close Officer Bo smells like fried eggs and gasoline, like breakfast at the Amoco.

"I'll put the word out with the other boys," he says. "Salinas here will be in his office. Why don't you go on back to your hotel room in case your daddy shows up there?"

Back in the room, I lie in my father's unmade bed. The sheets smell like his cologne, an odd mix of lavender and lime that I've always thought too pungent, but that he likes nonetheless.

I jump up when I hear the click from the electronic key in the door. It's the maid. She's a young Cuban woman who is overly polite, making up for her lack of English with deferential gestures: a great big smile, a nod, even a bow as she backs out of the room. She reminds me of my mother when she has to work on non-Haitian clients at her beauty shop, how she pays much more attention to those clients, forcing herself to laugh at jokes she barely understands and smiling at insults she doesn't quite grasp, all to avoid being forced into a conversation, knowing she couldn't hold up her end very well.

It's almost noon when I pick up the phone and call my mother at the salon. One of her employees tells me that she's not yet returned from the Mass she attends every day. After the Mass, if she has clients waiting, she'll walk the twenty blocks from the church to the salon. If she has no appointments, then she'll let her workers handle the walk-ins and go home for lunch. This was as close to retirement as my mother would ever come. This routine was her dream when she first started the shop. She had always wanted a life with room for daily Mass and long walks and the option of sometimes not going to work.

I call my parents' house. My mother isn't there either, so I leave the hotel number on the machine.

"Please call as soon as you can, Manman," I say. "It's about Papa."

It's early afternoon when my mother calls back, her voice cracking with worry. I had been sitting in that tiny hotel room, eating chips and candy bars from the vending ma-

chines, chain-smoking and waiting for something to happen, either for my father, Officer Bo, or Manager Salinas
to walk into the room with some terrible news or for my
mother or Gabrielle Fonteneau to call. I took turns imagining my mother screaming hysterically, berating both
herself and me for thinking this trip with my father a good
idea, then envisioning Gabrielle Fonteneau calling to say
that we shouldn't have come on the trip. It had all been a
joke. She wasn't going to buy a sculpture from me after all,
especially one I didn't have.

"Where Papa?" Just as I expected, my mother sounds as
though she's gasping for breath. I tell her to calm down,
that nothing bad has happened. Papa's okay. I've just lost
sight of him for a little while.

"How you lost him?" she asks.

"He got up before I did and disappeared," I say.

"How long he been gone?"

I can tell she's pacing back and forth in the kitchen, her
slippers flapping against the Mexican tiles. I can hear the
faucet when she turns it on, imagine her pushing a glass
underneath it and filling it up. I hear her sipping the water
as I say, "He's been gone for hours now. I don't even
believe it myself."

"You call police?"

Now she's probably sitting at the kitchen table, her eyes
closed, her fingers sliding back and forth across her forehead. She clicks her tongue and starts humming one of
those mournful songs from the Mass, songs that my father,

who attends church only at Christmas, picks up from her and also hums to himself in the shower.

My mother stops humming just long enough to ask, "What the police say?"

"To wait, that he'll come back."

There's a loud tapping on the line, my mother thumping her fingers against the phone's mouthpiece; it gives me a slight ache in my ear.

"He come back," she says with more certainty than either Officer Bo or Manager Salinas. "He not leave you like that."

I promise to call my mother hourly with an update, but I know she'll call me sooner than that, so I dial Gabrielle Fonteneau's cell phone. Gabrielle Fonteneau's voice sounds just as it does on television, but more silken, nuanced, and seductive without the sitcom laugh track.

"To think," my father once said while watching her show, in which she plays a smart-mouthed nurse in an inner-city hospital's maternity ward. "A Haitian-born actress with her own American television show. We have really come far."

"So nice of you to come all this way to personally deliver the sculpture," Gabrielle Fonteneau says. She sounds like she's in a place with cicadas, waterfalls, palm trees, and citronella candles to keep the mosquitoes away. I realize that I too am in such a place, but I'm not able to enjoy it.

"Were you told why I like this sculpture so much?" Gabrielle Fonteneau asks. "It's regal and humble at the same time. It reminds me of my own father."

I hadn't been trying to delve into the universal world of fathers, but I'm glad my sculpture reminds Gabrielle Fonteneau of her father, for I'm not beyond the spontaneous fanaticism inspired by famous people, whose breezy declarations seem to carry so much more weight than those of ordinary mortals. I still had trouble believing I had Gabrielle Fonteneau's cell number, which Céline Benoit had made me promise not to share with anyone else, not even my father.

My thoughts are drifting from Gabrielle Fonteneau's father to mine when I hear her say, "So when will you get here? You have the directions, right? Maybe you can join us for lunch tomorrow, at around twelve."

"We'll be there," I say.

But I'm no longer so certain.

My father loves museums. When he's not working at his barbershop, he's often at the Brooklyn Museum. The Ancient Egyptian rooms are his favorites.

"The Egyptians, they was like us," he likes to say. The Egyptians worshiped their gods in many forms, fought among themselves, and were often ruled by foreigners. The pharaohs were like the dictators he had fled, and their queens were as beautiful as Gabrielle Fonteneau. But what he admires most about the Ancient Egyptians is the way they mourn their dead.

"They know how to grieve," he'd say, marveling at the

mummification process that went on for weeks but resulted in corpses that survived thousands of years.

My whole adult life, I have struggled to find the proper manner of sculpting my father, a quiet and distant man who only came alive while standing with me most of the Saturday mornings of my childhood, mesmerized by the golden masks, the shawabtis, and the schist tablets, Isis, Nefertiti, and Osiris, the jackal-headed ruler of the underworld.

The sun is setting and my mother has called more than a dozen times when my father finally appears in the hotel room doorway. He looks like a much younger man and appears calm and rested, as if bronzed after a long day at the beach.

"Too smoky in here," he says.

I point to my makeshift ashtray, a Dixie cup filled with tobacco-dyed water and cigarette butts.

"Ka, let your father talk to you." He fans the smoky air with his hands, walks over to the bed, and bends down to unlace his sneakers. "Yon ti koze, a little chat."

"Where were you?" I feel my eyelids twitching, a nervous reaction I inherited from my epileptic mother. "Why didn't you leave a note? And Papa, where is the sculpture?"

"That is why we must chat," he says, pulling off his sand-filled sneakers and rubbing the soles of his large, calloused feet each in turn. "I have objections."

He's silent for a long time, concentrating on his foot massage, as though he'd been looking forward to it all day.

"I'd prefer you not sell that statue," he says at last. Then he turns away, picks up the phone, and calls my mother.

"I know she called you," he says to her in Creole. "She panicked. I was just walking, thinking."

I hear my mother loudly scolding him, telling him not to leave me again. When he hangs up, he grabs his sneakers and puts them back on.

"Where's the sculpture?" My eyes are twitching so badly now I can barely see.

"We go," he says. "I take you to it."

We walk out to the parking lot, where the hotel sprinkler is once more at work, spouting water onto the grass and hedges like centrifugal rain. The streetlights are on now, looking brighter and brighter as the dusk deepens around them. New hotel guests are arriving. Others are leaving for dinner, talking loudly as they walk to their cars.

As my father maneuvers our car out of the parking lot, I tell myself that he might be ill, mentally ill, even though I'd never detected any signs of it before, beyond his prison nightmares.

When I was eight years old and my father had the measles for the first time in his life, I overheard him say to a customer on the phone, "Maybe serious. Doctor tell me, at my age, measles can kill."

This was the first time I realized that my father could

die. I looked up the word "kill" in every dictionary and encyclopedia at school, trying to understand what it really meant, that my father could be eradicated from my life.

My father stops the car on the side of the highway near a man-made lake, one of those marvels of the modern tropical city, with curved stone benches surrounding a stagnant body of water. There's scant light to see by except a half-moon. Stomping the well-manicured grass, my father heads toward one of the benches. I sit down next to him, letting my hands dangle between my legs.

Here I am a little girl again, on some outing with my father, like his trips to the botanic garden or the zoo or the Egyptian statues at the museum. Again, I'm there simply because he wants me to be. I knew I was supposed to learn something from these childhood outings, but it took me years to realize that ultimately my father was doing his best to be like other fathers, to share as much of himself with me as he could.

I glance over at the lake. It's muddy and dark, and there are some very large pink fishes bobbing back and forth near the surface, looking as though they want to leap out and trade places with us.

"Is this where the sculpture is?" I ask.

"In the water," he says.

"Okay," I say calmly. But I know I'm already defeated. I know the piece is already lost. The cracks have probably taken in so much water that the wood has split into several chunks and plunged to the bottom. All I can think of saying is something glib, something I'm not even sure my father will understand.

"Please know this about yourself," I say. "You're a very harsh critic."

My father attempts to smother a smile. He scratches his chin and the scar on the side of his face, but says nothing. In this light the usually chiseled and embossed-looking scar appears deeper than usual, yet somehow less threatening, like a dimple that's spread out too far.

Anger is a wasted emotion, I've always thought. My parents would complain to each other about unjust politics in New York, but they never got angry at my grades, at all the Cs I got in everything but art classes, at my not eating my vegetables or occasionally vomiting my daily spoonful of cod-liver oil. Ordinary anger, I've always thought, is useless. But now I'm deeply angry. I want to hit my father, beat the craziness out of his head.

"Ka," he says, "I tell you why I named you Ka."

Yes, he'd told me, many, many times before. Now does not seem like a good time to remind me, but maybe he's hoping it will calm me, keep me from hating him for the rest of my life.

"Your mother not like the name at all," he says. "She say everybody tease you, people take pleasure repeating your name, calling you Kaka, Kaka, Kaka."

This too I had heard before.

"Okay," I interrupt him with a quick wave of my hands. "I've got it."

"I call you Ka," he says, "because in Egyptian world—"

A ka is a double of the body, I want to complete the sentence for him—the body's companion through life and after life. It guides the body through the kingdom of the dead. That's what I tell my students when I overhear them referring to me as Teacher Kaka.

"You see, ka is like soul," my father now says. "In Haiti is what we call good angel, ti bon anj. When you born, I look at your face, I think, here is my ka, my good angel."

I'm softening a bit. Hearing my father call me his good angel is the point at which I often stop being apathetic.

"I say rest in Creole," he prefaces, "because my tongue too heavy in English to say things like this, especially older things."

"Fine," I reply defiantly in English.

"Ka," he continues in Creole, "when I first saw your statue, I wanted to be buried with it, to take it with me into the other world."

"Like the Ancient Egyptians," I continue in English.

He smiles, grateful, I think, that in spite of everything, I can still appreciate his passions.

"Ka," he says, "when I read to you, with my very bad accent, from *The Book of the Dead*, do you remember how I made you read some chapters to me too?"

But this recollection is harder for me to embrace. I had been terribly bored by *The Book of the Dead*. The images of dead hearts being placed on scales and souls traveling aimlessly down fiery underground rivers had given me my own nightmares. It had seemed selfish of him not to ask me what I wanted to listen to before going to bed, what I wanted to read and have read to me. But since he'd recovered from the measles and hadn't died as we'd both feared, I'd vowed to myself to always tolerate, even indulge him, letting him take me places I didn't enjoy and read me things I cared nothing about, simply to witness the joy they gave him, the kind of bliss that might keep a dying person alive. But maybe he wasn't going to be alive for long. Maybe this is what *this* outing is about. Perhaps my "statue," as he called it, is a sacrificial offering, the final one that he and I would make together before he was gone.

"Are you dying?" I ask my father. It's the one explanation that would make what he's done seem insignificant or even logical. "Are you ill? Are you going to die?"

What would I do now, if this were true? I'd find him the best doctor, move back home with him and my mother. I'd get a serious job, find a boyfriend, and get married, and I'd never complain again about his having dumped my sculpture in the lake.

Like me, my father tends to be silent a moment too long during an important conversation and then say too much when less should be said. I listen to the wailing of crickets and cicadas, though I can't tell where they're coming from. There's the highway, and the cars racing by, the half-moon, the lake dug up from the depths of the ground—with my sculpture now at the bottom of it, the allée of royal palms whose shadows intermingle with the giant fishes on the surface of that lake, and there is me and my father.

"Do you recall the judgment of the dead," my father

speaks up at last, "when the heart of a person is put on a scale? If it's heavy, the heart, then this person cannot enter the other world."

It is a testament to my upbringing, and perhaps the Kaka and good angel story has something to do with this as well, that I remain silent now, at this particular time.

"I don't deserve a statue," my father says. But at this very instant he does look like one, like the Madonna of humility, contemplating her losses in the dust, or an Ancient Egyptian funerary priest, kneeling with his hands prayerfully folded on his lap.

"Ka," he says, "when I took you to the Brooklyn Museum, I would stand there for hours admiring them. But all you noticed was how there were pieces missing from them, eyes, noses, legs, sometimes even heads. You always noticed more what was not there than what was."

Of course, this way of looking at things was why I ultimately began sculpting in the first place, to make statues that would amaze my father even more than these ancient relics.

"Ka, I am like one of those statues," he says.

"An Ancient Egyptian?" I hear echoes of my loud, derisive laugh only after I've been laughing for a while. It's the only weapon I have now, the only way I know to take my revenge on my father.

"Don't do that," he says, frowning, irritated, almost shouting over my laughter. "Why do that? If you are mad, let yourself be mad. Why do you always laugh like a clown when you are angry?"

I tend to wave my hands about wildly when I laugh, but I don't notice I'm doing that now until he reaches over to grab them. I quickly move them away, but he ends up catching my right wrist, the same wrist Officer Bo had stroked earlier to make me shut up. My father holds on to it so tightly now that I feel his fingers crushing the bone, almost splitting it apart, and I can't laugh anymore.

"Let go," I say, and he releases my wrist quickly. He looks down at his own fingers, then lowers his hand to his lap.

My wrist is still throbbing. I keep stroking it to relieve some of the pain. It's the ache there that makes me want to cry more than anything, not so much this sudden, uncharacteristic flash of anger from my father.

"I'm sorry," he says. "I did not want to hurt you. I did not want to hurt anyone."

I keep rubbing my wrist, hoping he'll feel even sorrier, even guiltier for grabbing me so hard, but even more for throwing away my work.

"Ka, I don't deserve a statue," he says again, this time much more slowly, "not a whole one, at least. You see, Ka, your father was the hunter, he was not the prey."

I stop stroking my wrist, sensing something coming that might hurt much more. He's silent again. I don't want to prod him, feed him any cues, urge him to speak, but finally I get tired of the silence and feel I have no choice but to ask, "What are you talking about?"

I immediately regret the question. Is he going to

explain why he and my mother have no close friends, why they've never had anyone over to the house, why they never speak of any relatives in Haiti or anywhere else, or have never returned there or, even after I learned Creole from them, have never taught me anything else about the country beyond what I could find out on my own, on the television, in newspapers, in books? Is he about to tell me why Manman is so pious? Why she goes to daily Mass? I am not sure I want to know anything more than the little they've chosen to share with me all these years, but it is clear to me that he needs to tell me, has been trying to for a long time.

"We have a proverb," he continues. "One day for the hunter, one day for the prey. Ka, your father was the hunter, he was not the prey."

Each word is now hard-won as it leaves my father's mouth, balanced like those hearts on the Ancient Egyptian scales.

"Ka, I was never in prison," he says.

"Okay," I say, sounding like I am fourteen again, chanting from what my mother used to call the meaningless adolescent chorus, just to sound like everyone else my age.

"I was working in the prison," my father says. And I decide not to interrupt him again until he's done.

Stranded in the middle of this speech now, he has to go on. "It was one of the prisoners inside the prison who cut my face in this way," he says.

My father now points to the long, pitted scar on his right cheek. I am so used to his hands covering it up that this new purposeful motion toward it seems dramatic and extreme, almost like raising a veil.

"This man who cut my face," he continues, "I shot and killed him, like I killed many people."

I'm amazed that he managed to say all of this in one breath, like a monologue. I wish I too had had some rehearsal time, a chance to have learned what to say in response.

There is no time yet, no space in my brain to allow for whatever my mother might have to confess. Was she huntress or prey? A thirty-year-plus disciple of my father's coercive persuasion? She'd kept to herself even more than he had, like someone who was nurturing a great pain that she could never speak about. Yet she had done her best to be a good mother to me, taking charge of feeding and clothing me and making sure my hair was always combed, leaving only what she must have considered my intellectual development to my father.

When I was younger, she'd taken me to Mass with her on Sundays. Was I supposed to have been praying for my father all that time, the father who was the hunter and not the prey?

I think back to "The Negative Confession" ritual from *The Book of the Dead*, a ceremony that was supposed to take place before the weighing of hearts, giving the dead a chance to affirm that they'd done only good things in their lifetime. It was one of the chapters my father read to me most often. Now he was telling me I should have heard something beyond what he was reading. I should have removed the negatives.

"I am not a violent man," he had read. "I have made no one weep. I have never been angry without cause. I have never uttered any lies. I have never slain any men or women. I have done no evil."

And just so I will be absolutely certain of what I'd heard, I ask my father, "And those nightmares you were always having, what were they?"

"Of what I," he says, "your father, did to others."

Another image of my mother now fills my head, of her as a young woman, a woman my age, taking my father in her arms. At what point did she decide that she loved him? When did she know that she was supposed to have despised him?

"Does Manman know?" I ask.

"Yes," he says. "I explained, after you were born."

I am the one who drives the short distance back to the hotel. The ride seems drawn out; the cars in front of us appear to be dawdling. I honk impatiently, even when everyone except me is driving at a normal speed. My father is silent, not even telling me, as he has always done whenever he's been my passenger, to calm down, to be careful, to take my time.

As we are pulling into the hotel parking lot, I realize that I haven't notified Officer Bo and Manager Salinas that my father has been found. I decide that I will call them from my room. Then, before we leave the car, my father says, "Ka, no matter what, I'm still your father, still your mother's husband. I would never do these things now."

And this to me is as meaningful a declaration as his other confession. It was my first inkling that maybe my father was wrong in his own representation of his former life, that maybe his past offered more choices than being either hunter or prey.

When we get back to the hotel room, I find messages from both Officer Bo and Manager Salinas. Their shifts are over, but I leave word informing them that my father has returned.

While I'm on the phone, my father slips into the bathroom and runs the shower at full force. He is not humming.

When it seems he's never coming out, I call my mother at home in Brooklyn.

"Manman, how do you love him?" I whisper into the phone.

My mother is clicking her tongue and tapping her fingers against the mouthpiece again. Her soft tone makes me think I have awakened her from her sleep.

"He tell you?" she asks.

"Yes," I say.

"Everything?"

"Is there more?"

"What he told you he want to tell you for long time," she says, "you, his good angel."

It has always amazed me how much my mother and father echo each other, in their speech, their actions, even in their businesses. I wonder how much more alike they could possibly be. But why shouldn't they be alike? Like all parents, they were a society of two, sharing a series of private codes and associations, a past that even if I'd been born in the country of their birth, I still wouldn't have known, couldn't have known, thoroughly. I was a part of them. Some might say I belonged to them. But I wasn't them.

"I don't know, Ka." My mother is whispering now, as though there's a chance she might also be overheard by my father. "You and me, we save him. When I meet him, it made him stop hurt the people. This how I see it. He a seed thrown in rock. You, me, we make him take root."

As my mother is speaking, this feeling comes over me that I sometimes have when I'm carving, this sensation that my hands don't belong to me at all, that something else besides my brain and muscles is moving my fingers, something bigger and stronger than myself, an invisible puppetmaster over whom I have no control. I feel as though it's this same puppetmaster that now forces me to lower the phone and hang up, in midconversation, on my mother.

As soon as I put the phone down, I tell myself that I could continue this particular conversation at will, in a few minutes, a few hours, a few days, even a few years. Whenever I'm ready.

My father walks back into the room, his thinning hair wet, his pajamas on. My mother does not call me back. Somehow she must know that she has betrayed me by not sharing my confusion and, on some level, my feeling that my life could have gone on fine without my knowing these types of things about my father.

When I get up the next morning, my father's already dressed. He's sitting on the edge of the bed, his head bowed, his face buried in his palms, his forehead shadowed by his fingers. If I were sculpting him at this moment, I would carve a praying mantis, crouching motionless, seeming to pray, while actually waiting to strike.

With his back to me now, my father says, "Will you call that actress and tell her we have it no more, the statue?"

"We were invited to lunch there," I say. "I believe we should go and tell her in person."

He raises his shoulders and shrugs.

"Up to you," he says.

We start out for Gabrielle Fonteneau's house after breakfast. It's not quite as hot as the previous morning, but it's getting there. I crank up the AC at full blast, making it almost impossible for us to have a conversation, even if we wanted to.

The drive seems longer than the twenty-four hours it took to get to Lakeland from New York. I quickly grow tired of the fake lakes, the fenced-in canals, the citrus groves, the fan-shaped travelers' palms, the highway so imposingly neat. My father turns his face away from me and takes in the tropical landscape, as though he will never see it again. I know he's enjoying the live oaks with Spanish moss and bromeliads growing in their shade, the yellow trumpet flowers and flame vines, the tamarinds and jacaranda trees we speed by, because he expressed his admiration for them before, on the first half of our journey.

As we approach Gabrielle Fonteneau's house, my father breaks the silence in the car by saying, "Now you see, Ka, why your mother and me, we have never returned home."

The Fonteneaus' house is made of bricks and white coral, on a cul-de-sac with a row of banyans separating the two sides of the street.

My father and I get out of the car and follow a concrete path to the front door. Before we can knock, an older woman appears in the doorway. It's Gabrielle Fonteneau's mother. She resembles Gabrielle Fonteneau, or the way Gabrielle looks on television, with stunning almond eyes, skin the color of sorrel and spiraling curls brushing the sides of her face.

"We've been looking out for you," she says with a broad smile.

When Gabrielle's father joins her in the doorway, I realize where Gabrielle Fonteneau gets her height. He's more than six feet tall.

Mr. Fonteneau extends his hands, first to my father and then to me. They're relatively small, half the size of my father's.

We move slowly through the living room, which has a cathedral ceiling and walls covered with Haitian paintings with subjects ranging from market scenes and first communions to weddings and wakes. Most remarkable is a life-size portrait of Gabrielle Fonteneau sitting on a canopy-covered bench in what seems like her parents' garden.

Out on the back terrace, which towers over a nursery of azaleas, hibiscus, dracaenas, and lemongrass, a table is set for lunch.

Mr. Fonteneau asks my father where he is from in Haiti, and my father lies. In the past, I thought he always said he was from a different province each time because he'd really lived in all of those places, but I realize now that he says this to reduce the possibility of anyone identifying him, even though thirty-seven years and a thinning head of widow-peaked salt-and-pepper hair shield him from the threat of immediate recognition.

When Gabrielle Fonteneau makes her entrance, in an off-the-shoulder ruby dress, my father and I both rise from our seats.

"Gabrielle," she coos, extending her hand to my father, who leans forward and kisses it before spontaneously blurting out, "My dear, you are one of the most splendid flowers of Haiti."

Gabrielle Fonteneau looks a bit flustered. She tilts her head coyly and turns toward me.

"Welcome," she says.

During the meal of conch, fried plantains, and mushroom rice, Mr. Fonteneau tries to draw my father into conversation by asking him, in Creole, when he was last in Haiti.

"Thirty-seven years," my father answers with a mouthful of food.

"No going back for you?" asks Mrs. Fonteneau.

"I have not yet had the opportunity," my father replies.

"We go back every year," says Mrs. Fonteneau, "to a beautiful place overlooking the ocean, in the mountains of Jacmel."

"Have you ever been to Jacmel?" Gabrielle Fonteneau asks me.

I shake my head no.

"We're fortunate," Mrs. Fonteneau says, "that we have a place to go where we can say the rain is sweeter, the dust is lighter, our beaches prettier."

"So now we are tasting rain and weighing dust?" Mr. Fonteneau says and laughs.

"There's nothing like drinking the sweet juice from a coconut fetched from your own tree." Mrs. Fonteneau's eyes are lit up now as she puts her fork down to better paint the picture for us. She's giddy; her voice grows louder and higher, and even her daughter is absorbed, smiling and recollecting with her mother.

"There's nothing like sinking your hand in sand from the beach in your own country," Mrs. Fonteneau is saying. "It's a wonderful feeling, wonderful."

I imagine my father's nightmares. Maybe he dreams of dipping his hands in the sand on a beach in his own country and finding that what he comes up with is a fistful of blood.

After lunch, my father asks if he can have a closer look at the Fonteneaus' garden. While he's taking the tour, I make my confession about the sculpture to Gabrielle Fonteneau.

She frowns as she listens, fidgeting, shifting her weight from one foot to the other, as though she's greatly annoyed that so much of her valuable time had been so carelessly squandered on me. Perhaps she's wondering if this was just an elaborate scheme to meet her, perhaps she wants us out of her house as quickly as possible.

"I don't usually have people come into my house like this," she says, "I promise you."

"I appreciate it," I say. "I'm grateful for your trust and I didn't mean to violate it."

"I guess if you don't have it, then you don't have it," she says. "But I'm very disappointed. I really wanted to give that piece to my father."

"I'm sorry," I say.

"I should have known something was off," she says, looking around the room, as if for something more interesting to concentrate on. "Usually when people come here to sell us art, first of all they're always carrying it with them and they always show it to us right away. But since you know Céline, I overlooked that."

"There was a sculpture," I say, aware of how stupid my excuse was going to sound. "My father didn't like it, and he threw it away."

She raises her perfectly arched eyebrows, as if out of concern for my father's sanity, or for my own. Or maybe it's another indirect signal that she now wants us out of her sight.

"We're done, then," she says, looking directly at my face. "I have to make a call. Enjoy the rest of your day."

Gabrielle Fonteneau excuses herself, disappearing behind a closed door. Through the terrace overlooking the garden, I see her parents guiding my father along rows of lemongrass. I want to call Gabrielle Fonteneau back and promise her that I will make her another sculpture, but I can't. I don't know that I will be able to work on anything for some time. I have lost my subject, the prisoner father I loved as well as pitied.

In the garden Mr. Fonteneau snaps a few sprigs of lemongrass from one of the plants, puts them in a plastic bag that Mrs. Fonteneau is holding. Mrs. Fonteneau hands the bag of lemongrass to my father.

Watching my father accept with a nod of thanks, I remember the chapter "Driving Back Slaughters" from *The*

Book of the Dead, which my father sometimes read to me to drive away my fear of imagined monsters. It was a chapter full of terrible lines like "My mouth is the keeper of both speech and silence. I am the child who travels the roads of yesterday, the one who has been wrought from his eye."

I wave to my father in the garden to signal that we should leave now, and he slowly comes toward me, the Fonteneaus trailing behind him.

With each step forward, he rubs the scar on the side of his face, and out of a strange reflex I scratch my face in the same spot.

Maybe the last person my father harmed had dreamed moments like this into my father's future, strangers seeing that scar furrowed into his face and taking turns staring at it and avoiding it, forcing him to conceal it with his hands, pretend it's not there, or make up some lie about it, to explain.

Out on the sidewalk in front of the Fonteneaus' house, before we both take our places in the car, my father and I wave good-bye to Gabrielle Fonteneau's parents, who are standing in their doorway. Even though I'm not sure they understood the purpose of our visit, they were more than kind, treating us as though we were old friends of their daughter's, which maybe they had mistaken us for.

As the Fonteneaus turn their backs to us and close their front door, I look over at my father, who's still smiling and waving. When he smiles the scar shrinks and nearly disappears into the folds of his cheek, which used to make me make wish he would never stop smiling.

Once the Fonteneaus are out of sight, my father reaches down on his lap and strokes the plastic bag with the lemongrass the Fonteneaus had given him. The car is already beginning to smell too much like lemongrass, like air freshener overkill.

"What will you use that for?" I ask.

"To make tea," he says, "for Manman and me."

I pull the car away from the Fonteneaus' curb, dreading the rest stops, the gas station, the midway hotels ahead for us. I wish my mother were here now, talking to us about some miracle she'd just heard about in a sermon at the Mass. I wish my sculpture were still in the trunk. I wish I hadn't met Gabrielle Fonteneau, that I still had that to look forward to somewhere else, sometime in the future. I wish I could give my father whatever he'd been seeking in telling me his secret. But my father, if anyone could, must have already understood that confessions do not lighten living hearts.

I had always thought that my father's only ordeal was that he'd left his country and moved to a place where everything from the climate to the language was so unlike his own, a place where he never quite seemed to fit in, never appeared to belong. The only thing I can grasp now, as I drive way beyond the speed limit down yet another highway, is why the unfamiliar might have been so comforting, rather than distressing, to my father. And why he has never wanted the person he was, is, permanently documented in any way. He taught himself to appreciate the enormous weight of permanent markers by learning about the Ancient Egyptians. He had gotten to know them, through their crypts and monuments, in a way that he wanted no one to know him, no one except my mother and me, we, who are now his kas, his good angels, his masks against his own face.

SEVEN

Next month would make it seven years since he'd last seen his wife. Seven—a number he despised but had discovered was a useful marker. There were seven days between paychecks, seven hours, not counting lunch, spent each day at his day job, seven at his night job. Seven was the last number in his age—thirty-seven. And now there were seven hours left before his wife was due to arrive. Maybe it would be more, with her having to wait for her luggage and then make it through the long immigration line and past customs to look for him in the crowd of welcoming faces on the other side of the sliding doors at JFK. That is, if the flight from Port-au-Prince wasn't delayed, as it often was, or canceled altogether.

He shared an apartment in the basement of a two-story house with two other men, Michel and Dany. To prepare for the reunion, he'd cleaned his room, thrown out some cherry-red rayon shirts he knew his wife would hate, and then climbed the splintered steps to the first floor to tell the landlady that his wife was coming.

The landlady was heavyset and plain, almost homely, with deep ridges on her wide forehead.

"I don't have a problem with your wife coming." She often closed her eyes while speaking, as if to accentuate the pauses between her words. "I just hope she's clean."

"She is clean," he said.

"We understand each other, then."

The kitchen was the only room in the main part of the house he'd ever seen. It was pine-scented, spotless, and the dishes were neatly organized behind glass cabinets.

"Did you tell the men?" she asked, while sticking a frozen dessert in her microwave.

"I told them," he said.

He was waiting for her to announce that she'd have to charge him extra. She and her husband had agreed to rent the room to one person—a man they'd probably taken for a bachelor—not two.

"A woman living down there with three men," the landlady said, removing the small pie from the microwave. "Maybe your wife will be uncomfortable."

He wanted to tell her that it wasn't up to her to decide whether or not his wife would be comfortable. But he had been prepared for this too, for some unpleasant remark about his wife. Actually, he was up there as much to give notice that he was looking for an apartment as to announce that his wife was coming. As soon as he found an apartment, he would be moving.

"Okay, then," she said, opening her silverware drawer. "Remember, you start the month, you pay the whole thing."

"Thank you very much, Madame," he said.

As he walked back downstairs, he scolded himself for calling her Madame. Why had he acted like a manservant who'd just been dismissed? It was one of those class things from home he still couldn't shake. On the other hand, if he addressed the woman respectfully, it wasn't because she had more money than he did or even because after five years in the same room he was still paying only two hundred and fifty dollars a month. He was only making a sacrifice for his wife.

After his conversation with the landlady, he decided to have a more thorough one with the men who occupied the other two small rooms in the basement. The day before his wife was to arrive, he went into the kitchen to see them. The fact that they were wearing only sheer-looking loose boxers as they stumbled about bleary-eyed concerned him.

"You understand, she's a woman," he told them. He was not worried that she would be tempted by their bony torsos, but if she was still as sensitive as he remembered, their near-nakedness might embarrass her.

The men understood.

"If it were my wife," Michel said, "I'd feel the same."

Dany simply nodded.

They had robes, Michel declared after a while. They would wear them when she got here.

They didn't have robes, all three men knew this, but Michel would buy some, out of respect for the wife.

Michel, the youngest of the three, had advised him to pretty up his room, to buy some silk roses, some decorative prints for the walls (no naked girls), and some vanilla incense, which would be more pleasing than the pine-scented air fresheners that the people upstairs liked so much.

Dany told him he would miss their evenings out together. In the old days, they had often gone dancing at the Rendez Vous, which was now the Cenegal nightclub. But they hadn't gone much since the place had become famous—a Haitian man named Abner Louima was arrested there, then beaten and sodomized at a nearby police station.

He told Dany not to mention those nights out again. His wife wasn't to know that he'd ever done anything but work his two jobs, as a night janitor at Medgar Evers College and a day janitor at Kings' County Hospital. And she was never to find out about those women who'd occasionally come home with him in the early-morning hours. Those women, most of whom had husbands, boyfriends, fiancés, and lovers in other parts of the world, never meant much to him anyway.

Michel, who had become a lay minister at a Baptist church near the Rendez Vouz and never danced there, laughed as he listened. "The cock can no longer crow," he said. "You might as well give the rest to Jesus."

"Jesus wouldn't know what to do with what's left of this man," Dany said.

Gone were the early-evening domino games. Gone was

the phone number he'd had for the last five years, ever since he'd had a telephone. (He didn't need other women calling him now.) And it was only as he stood in the crowd of people waiting to meet the flights arriving simultaneously from Kingston, Santo Domingo, and Port-au-Prince that he stopped worrying that he might not see any delight or recognition in his wife's face. There, he began to feel some actual joy, even exhilaration, which made him want to leap forward and grab every woman who vaguely resembled the latest pictures she'd sent him, all of which he had neatly framed and hung on the walls of his room.

*   *   *

They were searching her suitcase. Why were they searching her suitcase? One meager bag, which, aside from some gifts for her husband, contained the few things she'd been unable to part with, the things her relatives hadn't nabbed from her, telling her that she could get more, and better, where she was going. She'd kept only her undergarments, a nightgown, and two outfits: the green princess dress she was wearing and a red jumper she'd gift-wrapped before packing so no one would take it. Neighbors who had traveled before had told her to gift-wrap everything so it wouldn't be reopened at the airport in New York. Now the customs man was tearing her careful wrapping to shreds as he barked questions at her in mangled Creole.

"Ki sa l ye?" He held a package out in front of her before unveiling it.

What was it? She didn't know anymore. She could only guess by the shapes and sizes.

The customs man unwrapped all her gifts—the mangoes, sugarcane, avocados, the grapefruit-peel preserves, the peanut, cashew, and coconut confections, the coffee beans, which he threw into a green bin decorated with fruits and vegetables with red lines across them. The only thing that seemed as though it might escape disposal was a small packet of trimmed chicken feathers, which her husband used to enjoy twirling in his ear cavity. In the early days, soon after he'd left, she had spun the tips of the feathers inside her ears too and discovered that from them she could get jwisans, pleasure, an orgasm. She'd thought then that maybe the foreign television programs were right: sex was mostly between the ears.

When the customs man came across the package of feathers, he stared down at it, then looked up at her, letting his eyes linger on her face, mostly, it seemed to her, on her ears. Clearly, he had seen feathers like these before. Into the trash they went, along with the rest of her offerings.

By the time he was done with her luggage, she had little left. The suitcase was so light now that she could walk very quickly as she carried it in one hand. She followed a man pushing a cart, which tipped and swerved under the weight of three large duffel bags. And suddenly she found herself before a door that slid open by itself, parting like a glass sea, and as she was standing there, blinking through the nearly blinding light shining down on the large number of people who had come to meet loved ones with flowers and placards and stuffed animals, the door closed again and when she moved a few steps forward it opened, and then she saw him. He charged at her and wrapped both his arms around her. And as he held her, she felt her feet leave the ground. It was when he put her back down that she finally believed she was really somewhere else, on another soil, in another country.

*   *   *

He could tell she was happy that so many of her pictures were displayed on the wall facing his bed. During the ride home, he had nearly crashed the car twice. He wasn't sure himself why he was driving so fast. They dashed through the small talk, the inventory of friends and family members, and the state of their health. She had no detailed anecdotes about anyone in particular. Some had died and some were still living; he couldn't even remember which. She was bigger than she had been when he left her, what people here might call chubby. It was obvious that she had been to a professional hairdresser, because she was elegantly coifed, with her short hair gelled down to her scalp and a fake bun bulging in the back. She smelled good, a mixture of lavender and lime. He simply wanted to get her home, if home it was, to that room, and to reduce the space between them until there was no air for her to breathe that he was not breathing too.

The drive reminded him of the one they had taken to their one-night honeymoon at the Ifé Hotel, when he had begged the uncle who was driving them to go faster, because the next morning he would be on a plane for New York. That night, he'd had no idea that it would be seven years before he would see her again. He'd had it all planned. He knew that he couldn't send for her right away, since he would be overstaying a tourist visa. But he was going to work hard, find a lawyer, get himself a green card, and then send for his wife. The green card had taken six years and eleven months. But now she was here with him, moving her face closer to her own pictures, squinting as her nose nearly touched the frames. It was as though she was looking at someone else.

"Do you remember that one?" he asked to reassure her. He was pointing at a framed eight-by-twelve of her lying on a red mat by a tiny Christmas tree in a photographer's studio. "You sent it last Noël?"

She remembered, she said. It was just that she looked so desperate, as if she were trying to force him to remember her by bombarding him with those photographs.

"I never forgot you for an instant," he said.

She said she was thirsty.

"What do you want to drink?" He listed the juices he had purchased from the Panamanian grocer down the street, the combinations he was sure she would be craving—papaya and mango, guava and pineapple, cherimoya and passion fruit.

"Just a little water," she said. "Cold."

He didn't want to leave her alone while he went to the kitchen. He would have called through the walls for one of the men to get some water, if only they were not doing such a good job of hiding behind the closed doors of their rooms to give him some previously requested privacy.

When he came back with the glass, she examined it, as if for dirt, and then gulped the water down. It was as though she hadn't drunk anything since the morning he had gotten on the plane and left her behind.

"Do you want more?" he asked.

She shook her head no.

It's too bad, he thought, that in Creole the word for love, renmen, is also the word for like, so that as he told her he loved her, he had to embellish it with phrases that illustrated the degree of that love. He loved her more than there were seconds in the seven years that they'd been apart, he babbled. He loved her more than the size of the ocean she'd just crossed. To keep himself from saying more insipid things, he jumped on top of her and pinned her down on the bed. She was not as timid as she had been on their wedding night. She tugged at his black tie so fiercely that he was sure his neck was bruised. He yanked a few buttons off her dress and threw them aside as she unbuttoned his starched and ironed white shirt, and though in the rehearsals in past daydreams he had gently placed a cupped hand over her mouth, he didn't think to do it now. He didn't care that the other men could hear them.

He was exhausted when she grabbed the top sheet from the bed, wrapped it around her, and announced she was going to the bathroom.

"Let me take you," he said.

"Non, non," she said. "I can find it."

He couldn't stand to watch her turn away and disappear.

He heard voices in the kitchen, her talking to the men, introducing herself. He bolted right up from the bed when he remembered that all she had on was the sheet. As he raced to the door, he collided with her coming back.

There were two men playing dominoes in the kitchen, she told him, dressed in identical pink satin robes.

• • •

He left early for work the next day, along with the other men, but not before handing her a set of keys and instructing her not to let anyone in. He showed her how to work the stove and how to find all the Haitian stations on the AM/FM dial of his night-table radio. She slept late, reliving the night, their laughter after she'd seen the men, who, he explained, had hurried to buy those robes for her benefit. They had made love again and again, forcing themselves to do so more quietly each time. Seven times, by his count— once for each year they'd been apart—but fewer by hers. He had assured her that there was no need to be embarrassed. They were married, before God and a priest. This was crucial for her to remember. That's why he had seen to it on the night before he left. So that something more judicial and committing than a mere promise would bind them. So that even if their union became a victim of distance and time, it couldn't be easily dissolved. They would have to sign papers to come apart, write letters, speak on the phone about it. He told her that he didn't want to leave her again, not for one second. But he had asked for the day off and his boss had refused. At least they would have the weekends, Saturdays and Sundays, to do with as they wished, to go dancing, sight-seeing, shopping, and apartment hunting. Wouldn't she like to have her own apartment? To make love as much as they wanted and not worry that some men in women's robes had heard them?

At noon, the phone rang. It was him. He asked her what she was doing. She lied and told him she was cooking, making herself something to eat. He asked what. She said eggs, guessing that there must be eggs in the refrigerator. He asked if she was bored. She said no. She was going to listen to the radio and write letters home.

When she hung up, she turned on the radio. She scrolled between the stations he had pointed out to her and was glad to hear people speaking Creole. There was music playing too, konpa, by a group named Top Vice. She switched to a station with a talk show and sat up to listen as some callers talked about a Haitian American man named Patrick Dorismond who'd been killed. He had been shot by a policeman in a place called Manhattan. She wanted to call her husband, but he hadn't left a number. Lying back, she raised the sheet over her head and through it listened to the callers, each one angrier than the last.

. . .

When he came home, he saw that she had used some of what she had found in the refrigerator and the kitchen cabinets to cook a large meal for all four of them. She insisted that they wait for the other men to drift in before they ate, even though he had only a few hours before he had to leave for his night job.

The men complimented her enthusiastically on her cooking, and he could tell that this meal made them feel as though they were part of a family, something they had not experienced for years. They seemed happy, eating for pleasure as well as sustenance, chewing more slowly than they ever had before. Usually they ate standing up, Chinese or Jamaican takeout from places down the street. Tonight there was little conversation, beyond praise for the food. The men offered to clean the pots and dishes once they were done, and he suspected that they wanted to lick them before washing them.

He and his wife went to the room and lay on their backs on the bed. He explained why he had two jobs. It had been partly to fill the hours away from her, but also partly because he had needed to support both himself here and her in Port-au-Prince. And now he was saving up for an apartment and, ultimately, a house. She said she too wanted to work. She had finished a secretarial course back home. Could that be helpful here? He warned her that because she didn't speak English, she might have to start as a cook in a Haitian restaurant or as a seamstress in a factory. He fell asleep in midthought. She woke him up at nine o'clock, when he was supposed to start work. He rushed to the bathroom to wash his face, came back, and changed his overalls, all the while cursing himself. He was stupid to have overslept, and now he was late.

He kissed her good-bye and ran out. He hated being late, being lectured by the night manager, whose favorite reprimand was, "There's tons of people like you in this city. Half of them need a job."

•   •   •

She spent the whole week inside, worried that she would get lost if she ventured out alone, that she might not be able to retrace her steps. Her days fell into a routine. She would wake up and listen to the radio for news of what was happening both here and back home. Somewhere, not far from where she was, people were in the streets, marching, protesting Dorismond's death, their outrage made even greater by the fact that the Dorismond boy was the American-born son of a well-known singer, whose voice they had heard on the radio back in Haiti.

"No justice, no peace," she chanted while stewing chicken and frying fish. In the afternoons, she wrote letters home. She wrote of the meals she made, of the pictures of her on the wall, of the songs and protest chants on the radio. She wrote to family members, and to childhood girlfriends who had been so happy that she was finally going to be with her husband, and to newer acquaintances from the secretarial school who had been so jealous. She also wrote to a male friend, a neighbor who had come to her house three days after her husband had left to see why she'd locked herself inside.

He had knocked for so long that she'd finally opened the door. She was still wearing the dress she had worn to see her husband off. When she collapsed in his arms, he put a cold compress on her forehead and offered her some water. She swallowed so much water so quickly that she vomited. That night, he lay down next to her, and in the dark told her that this was love, if love there was, having the courage to abandon the present for a future one could only imagine. He assured her that her husband loved her.

She wanted to tell her husband about that neighbor who had slept next to her those days after he'd left and in whose bed she had spent many nights after that. Only then would she feel like their future would be true. Someone had said that people lie only at the beginning of relationships. The middle is where the truth resides. But there had been no middle for her husband and herself, just a beginning and many dream-rehearsed endings.

• • •

He had first met his wife during carnival in a seaside town in Jacmel. His favorite part of the festivities was the finale, on the day before Ash Wednesday, when a crowd of tired revelers would gather on the beach to burn their carnival masks and costumes and feign weeping, symbolically purging themselves of the carousing of the preceding days and nights. She had volunteered to be one of the official weepers, one of those who wailed most convincingly as the carnival relics turned to ashes in the bonfire.

"Papa Kanaval ou ale! Farewell Father Carnival!" she howled, with real tears running down her face.

If she could grieve so passionately on demand, he thought, perhaps she could love even more. After the other weepers had left, she stayed behind until the last embers of the carnival bonfire had dimmed. It was impossible to distract her, to make her laugh. She could never fake weeping, she told him. Every time she cried for anything, she cried for everything else that had ever hurt her.

He had traveled between Jacmel and Port-au-Prince while he was waiting for his visa to come through. And when he finally had a travel date he asked her to marry him.

One New York afternoon, when he came home from work, he found her sitting on the edge of the bed in that small room, staring at the pictures of herself on the opposite wall. She didn't move as he kissed the top of her head. He said nothing, simply slipped out of his clothes and lay down on the bed, pressing his face against her back. He did not want to trespass on her secrets. He simply wanted to extinguish the carnivals burning in her head.

• • •

She was happy when the weekend finally came. Though he slept until noon, she woke up at dawn, rushed to the bathroom to get there before the men could, put on her red jumper and one of his T-shirts, then sat staring down at him on the bed, waiting for his eyes to open.

"What plan do we have for today?" she asked when they finally did.

The plan, he said, was whatever she wanted.

She wanted to walk down a street with him and see faces. She wanted to eat something, an apple or a chicken leg, out in the open with the sun beating down on her face.

As they were leaving the house, they came across the landlady, who was standing between two potted bouquets of white carnations on her front steps. She nodded politely to the landlady, then pulled her husband away by the hand. They walked down a street filled with people doing their Saturday food shopping at outside stalls stacked with fruits and vegetables.

He asked if she wanted to take the bus.

"Where to?"

"Anywhere," he said.

From the bus, she counted the frame and row houses, beauty shop signs, church steeples, and gas stations. She pressed her face against the window, and her breath occasionally blocked her view of the streets speeding by. She turned back now and then to look at him sitting next to her. There was still a trace of sleepiness in his eyes. He watched her as though he were trying to put himself in her place, to see it all as if for the first time, but he could not.

He took her to a park in the middle of Brooklyn, Prospect Park, a vast stretch of land, trees, and trails. They strolled deep into the park, until they could see only a few of the surrounding buildings, which towered like mountains above the city landscape. In all her daydreams she had never imagined that there would be a place like this here. This immense garden, he told her, was where he came to ponder seasons, lost time, and interminable distances.

• • •

It was past seven o'clock when they emerged from the park and headed down Parkside Avenue. She had reached for his hand at 5:11 p.m., he had noted, and had not released it since. And now as they were walking down a dimly lit side street, she kept her eyes upward, looking into the windows of apartments lit by the indigo glow of television screens.

When she said she was hungry, they walked down Flatbush Avenue in search of something to eat. Walking hand in hand with her through crowds of strangers made him long for his other favorite piece of Jacmel carnival theater. A bride and groom, in their most lavish wedding clothing, would wander the streets. Scanning a crowd of revelers, they'd pick the most stony-faced person and ask, "Would you marry us?"

Over the course of several days, for variety, they'd modify this request. "Would you couple us?" "Would you make us one?" "Would you tie the noose of love around our necks?"

The joke was that when the person took the bait and looked closely, he or she might discover that the bride was a man and the groom a woman. The couple's makeup was so skillfully applied and their respective outfits so well fitted that only the most observant revelers could detect this.

• • •

On the nearly empty bus on the way home, he sat across the aisle from her, not next to her as he had that morning. She pretended to keep her eyes on the night racing past the window behind him. He was watching her again. This time he seemed to be trying to see *her* as if for the first time, but he could not.

She too was thinking of carnival and of how the year after they'd met they had dressed as a bride and groom looking for someone to marry them. She had disguised herself as the bride and he as the groom, forgoing the traditional puzzle.

At the end of the celebrations, she had burned her wedding dress in the bonfire and he had burned his suit. She wished now that they had kept them. They could have walked these foreign streets in them, performing their own carnival. Since she didn't know the language, they wouldn't have to speak or ask any questions of the stony-faced people around them. They could carry out their public wedding march in silence, a temporary silence, unlike the one that had come over them now.

WATER CHILD

The letter came on the first of the month, as usual. It was written, as most of them were, in near-calligraphic style, in blue ink, on see-through airmail paper.

> Ma chère Nadine,
> We are so happy to have this occasion to put pen to paper to write to you. How are you? All is well with us, grace à Dieu, except your father whose health is, as always, unreliable. Today it is his knees. Tomorrow it will be something else. You know how it is when you are old. He and I both thank you for the money you sent last month. We know it is difficult for you, but we are very grateful. This month your father hopes to see yet another doctor. We have not heard your voice in a while and our ears long for it. Please telephone us.

It was signed, "Your mother and father who embrace you very tightly."

. . .

Three weeks had gone by since the letter arrived, and Nadine still hadn't called. She had raided her savings to wire double the usual amount but hadn't called. Instead she took the letter out each day as she ate a tuna melt for lunch in the hospital cafeteria, where each first Friday for the last three years she had added a brownie to her meal for scheduled variety.

Every time she read the letter, she tried to find something else between the lines, a note of sympathy, commiseration, condolence. But it simply wasn't there. The more time went by, the more brittle and fragile the letter became. Each time she held the paper between her fingers she wondered how her mother had not torn it with the pen she'd used to compose each carefully inscribed word. How had the postal workers in both Port-au-Prince and Brooklyn not lacerated the thin page and envelope? And how had the letter not turned to dust in her purse during her bus ride to and from work? Or while rubbing against the inner lining of the left pocket of her nursing uniform, where she kept it all day long?

She carefully folded the letter once again and replaced it in her pocket as one of her colleagues approached the corner table by the window that she occupied in solitude for a whole hour each working day. Josette kissed her on both cheeks while fumbling in her own pocket for lunch money. As Nadine's lunch hour was winding down, Josette's was just beginning.

Nadine smiled to herself at this ability of Josette's to make an ordinary encounter feel so intimate, then turned her face to the view outside, to the brown buildings and their barred windows. She let her eyes linger on the nursing station of the Psych ward across the alley and entertained a vision she often had of seeing a patient dive out of one of the windows.

"Ms. Hinds is back from ICU," Josette was saying. "She's so upset and sezi that Doctor Vega had to give her a sedative."

Nadine and Josette worked different ends of Ear, Nose, and Throat and saw many post-op patients wake up bewildered to discover that their total laryngectomies meant they would no longer be able to talk. No matter how the doctors, nurses, and counselors prepared them, it was still a shock.

Josette always gave Nadine a report on the patients whenever she came to take over the table. She was one of the younger Haitian RNs, one of those who had come to Brooklyn in early childhood and spoke English with no accent at all, but she liked to throw in a Creole word here and there in conversation to flaunt her origins. Aside from the brief lunch encounters, and times when one or the other needed a bit of extra help with a patient, they barely spoke at all.

"I am going now," Nadine said, rising from her seat. "My throne is yours."

. . .

When she returned to her one-bedroom condo in Canarsie that evening, Nadine was greeted by voices from the large television set that she kept on twenty-four hours a day. Along with the uneven piles of newspapers and magazines scattered between the fold-out couch and the floor-to-ceiling bookshelves in her living room, the television was her way of bringing voices into her life that required neither reaction nor response. At thirty, she'd tried other hobbies—African dance and drawing classes, Internet surfing—but these tasks had demanded either too much effort or too much superficial interaction with other people.

She took off the white sneakers that she wore at work and remained standing to watch the last ten minutes of a news broadcast. It wasn't until a game show began that she pressed the playback button on her blinking answering machine.

Her one message was from Eric, her former beau, suitor, lover, the near father of her nearly born child.

"Alo, allo, hello," he stammered, creating his own odd pauses between Creole, French, and English, like the electively mute, newly arrived immigrant children whose worried parents brought them to the ward for consultations, even though there was nothing wrong with their vocal cords.

"Just saying hello to you." He chose heavily accented English. Long pause. "Okay. Bye."

Whenever he called her now, which was about once a month since their breakup, she removed the microcassette from the answering machine and placed it on the altar she had erected on top of the dresser in her bedroom. It wasn't anything too elaborate. There was a framed drawing that she had made of a cocoa-brown, dewy-eyed baby that could as easily have been a boy as a girl, the plump, fleshy cheeks resembling hers and the high forehead resembling his. Next to the plain wooden frame were a dozen now dried red roses that Eric had bought her as they'd left the clinic after the procedure. She had once read about a shrine to unborn children in Japan, where water was poured over altars of stone to honor them, so she had filled her favorite drinking glass with water and a pebble and had added that to her own shrine, along with a total of now seven microcassettes with messages from Eric, messages she had never returned.

That night, as the apartment seemed oddly quiet in spite of the TV voices, she took out her mother's letter for its second reading of the day, ran her fingers down the delicate page, and reached for the phone to dial her parents' number. She'd almost called many times in the last three months, but had lost her nerve, thinking her voice might betray all that she could not say. She nearly dialed the whole thing this time. There were only a few numbers left when she put the phone down, tore the letter into two, then four, then eight, then countless pieces, collapsed among her old magazines and newspapers, and wept.

Another letter arrived at Nadine's house a week later. It was on the same kind of airmail paper, but this time the words were meticulously typed. The *a*s and *o*s, which had been struck over many times, created underlayers, shadows, and small holes within the vowels' perimeters.

> Ma chère Nadine,
> Your father and I thank you very much for the extra money. Your father used it to see a doctor, not about his knees, but his prostate that the doctor says is inflamed. Not to worry, he was given some medications and it seems as if he will be fine for a while. All the tests brought us short for the monthly expenses, but we will manage. We would like so much to talk to you. We wait every Sunday afternoon, hoping you will return to our beautiful routine. We pray that we have not abused your generosity, but you are our only child and we only ask for what we need. You know how it is when you are old. We have tried to telephone you, but we are always greeted by your répondeur, which will not accept collect calls. In any case, we wait to hear from you.
> Your mother and father who embrace you very tightly.

The next day, Nadine ignored her tuna melt altogether to read the letter over many times. She did not even notice the lunch hour pass. Josette arrived sooner than she expected. Josette, like all the other nurses, knew not to ask any questions about Nadine's past, present, future, or her international-looking mail. Word circulated quickly from old employees to new arrivals that Nadine Osnac was not a friendly woman. Anyone who had sought detailed conversations with her, or who had shown interest in sharing the table while she was sitting there, had met only with cold silence and a blank stare out to the Psych ward. Josette, however, still occasionally ventured a social invitation, since they were both from the same country and all.

"Some of the girls are going to the city after work," Josette was saying. "A little banbòch to celebrate Ms. Hinds' discharge tomorrow."

"No thanks," Nadine said, departing from the table a bit more abruptly than usual.

That same afternoon, Ms. Hinds began throwing things across her small private room, one of the few in the ward. Nadine nearly took a flower vase in the face as she rushed in to help. Unlike most of the patients in the ward, who were middle-aged or older, Ms. Hinds was a twenty-five-year-old nonsmoker.

When Nadine arrived, Ms. Hinds was thrashing about so much that the nurses, worried that she would yank out the metal tube inserted in her neck and suffocate, were trying to pin her down to put restraints on her arms and legs. Nadine quickly joined in the struggle, assigning herself Ms. Hinds' right arm, pockmarked from weeks of IVs in hard-to-conquer veins.

"Where's Doctor Vega?" Josette shouted as she caught one of Ms. Hinds' random kicks in her chest. Nadine lost her grip on the IV arm. She was looking closely at Ms. Hinds' face, her eyes tightly shut beneath where her eye-

brows used to be, her thinner lower lip protruding defiantly past her upper one as though she were preparing to
spit long distance in a contest, her whole body hairless
under the cerulean-blue hospital gown, which came with
neither a bonnet nor a hat to protect her now completely
bald head.

"The doctor's on his way," one of the male nurses said.
He had a firm hold of Ms. Hinds' left leg, but couldn't pin
it down to the bed long enough to restrain it.

"Leave her alone," Nadine shouted to the others.

One by one, the nurses each took a few steps back,
releasing Ms. Hinds' extremities. With her need to struggle suddenly gone, Ms. Hinds curled into a fetal position
and sank into the middle of the bed.

"Let me be alone with her," Nadine said in a much softer
voice.

The others lingered a while, as if not wanting to leave,
but they had other patients to see to, so, one at a time,
they backed out the door.

Nadine lowered the bed rail to give Ms. Hinds a sense
of freedom, even if limited.

"Ms. Hinds, is there something you want?" she asked.

Ms. Hinds opened her mouth wide, trying to force air
past her lips, but all that came out was the hiss of oxygen
and mucus filtering through the tube in her neck.

Nadine looked over at the night table, where there
should have been a pad and pen, but Ms. Hinds had
knocked them onto the floor with the magazines her parents had brought for her. She walked over and picked up

the pad and pen and pushed them toward Ms. Hinds, who was still lying in a ball in the middle of the bed.

Looking puzzled, Ms. Hinds turned her face toward Nadine, slowly unwrapping her body from around itself.

"I'm here, Ms. Hinds," Nadine said, now holding the pad within a few inches of Ms. Hinds' face. "Go ahead."

Ms. Hinds held out the gaunt fingers of her right hand. The fingers came apart slowly; then Ms. Hinds extended the whole hand, grabbing the pad. She had to force herself to sit up in order to write and she grimaced as she did so, trying to maintain her grip on the pad and slide up against the pillow Nadine propped behind her back.

Ms. Hinds scribbled down a few quick words, then held up the pad for Nadine to read. At first Nadine could not understand the handwriting. It was unsteady and hurried and the words ran together, but Nadine sounded them out, one letter at a time, with some encouragement from Ms. Hinds, who slowly moved her head up and down when Nadine guessed correctly.

"I can't speak," Nadine made out.

"That's right," Nadine said. "You can't."

Looking even more perplexed at Nadine's unsympathetic reaction, Ms. Hinds grabbed the pad from Nadine's hand and scribbled, "I'm a teacher."

"I know," Nadine said.

"WHY SEND ME HOME LIKE THIS?" Ms. Hinds scribbled next.

"Because we have done all we can for you here," Nadine said. "Now you must work with a speech therapist. You

can get an artificial larynx, a voice box. The speech therapist will help you."

"Feel like a basenji," Ms. Hinds wrote, her face sinking
closer to her chest.

"What's a b-a-s-e-n-j-i?" Nadine asked, spelling out the
word.

"A dog," Ms. Hinds wrote. "Doesn't bark."

"A dog that doesn't bark?" Nadine asked. "What kind of
dog is that?"

"Exists," Ms. Hinds wrote, as she bit down hard on her
quivering lower lip.

That night at home, Nadine found herself more exhausted
than usual. With the television news as white noise, she
dialed Eric's home phone number, hoping she was finally
ready to hear his voice for more than the twenty-five seconds her answering machine allowed. He should be home
resting now, she thought, preparing to start his second job
as a night janitor at Medgar Evers College.

Her mind was suddenly blank. What would she say?
She was trying to think of something frivolous, a line of
small talk, when she heard the message that his number
had been changed to one that was unlisted.

She quickly hung up and redialed, only to get the same
message. After dialing a few more times, she decided to
call her parents instead.

Ten years ago her parents had sold everything they
owned and moved from what passed for a lower-middle-

class neighborhood to one on the edge of a slum, in order to send her to nursing school abroad. Ten years ago she'd dreamed of seeing the world, of making her own way in it. These were the intangibles she'd proposed to her mother, the kindergarten teacher, and her father, the camion driver, in the guise of a nursing career. This was what they'd sacrificed everything for. But she always knew that she would repay them. And she had, with half her salary every month, and sometimes more. In return, what she got was the chance to parent them rather than have them parent her. Calling them, however, on the rare occasions that she actually called rather than received their calls, always made her wish to be the one guarded, rather than the guardian, to be reassured now and then that some wounds could heal, that some decisions would not haunt her forever.

"Manman," her voice immediately dropped to a whisper when her mother's came over the phone line, squealing with happiness.

For every decibel Nadine's voice dropped, her mother's rose. "My love, we were so worried about you. How are you? We have not heard your voice in so long."

"I'm fine, Manman," she said.

"You sound low. You sound down. We have to start planning again when you can come or when we can come see you, as soon as Papa can travel."

"How is Papa?" she asked.

"He's right here. Let me put him on. He'll be very glad to hear you."

Suddenly her father was on the phone, his tone calmer but excited in his own way. "We were waiting so long for this call, chérie."

"I know, Papa. I've been working really hard."

They never spoke of difficult things during these phone calls, of money or illnesses or doctors' visits. Papa always downplayed his aches and pains, which her mother would highlight in the letters. Events were relayed briefly, a list of accomplishments, no discussion of failures or losses, which could spoil moods for days, weeks, and months, until the next phone call.

"Do you have a boyfriend?" Her mother took back the phone. Nadine could imagine her skipping around their living room like a child's ball bouncing. "Is there anyone in your life?"

"No, Manman," she said.

"Don't wait too long," her mother said. "You don't want to be old alone."

"All right, Manman."

"Papa and I saw a kolibri today." Her mother liked moving from one subject to another. Her parents loved birds, especially hummingbirds, and never failed to report a sighting to her. Since every schoolboy made it his mission to slingshot hummingbirds to death, she was amazed that there were any left in Port-au-Prince, especially in her parents' neighborhood.

"It was just a little one," her mother was saying. "Very small."

She could hear her father add, "It's very clever. I think it's going to last. It loves our new hibiscus."

"You have hibiscus?" Nadine asked.

"Just a hedge," her mother said. "It's just starting to blossom. It brings us bees too, but I wouldn't say we have a hive."

"That's nice, Manman," she said. "I have to go now."

"So soon?"

"Please say good night to Papa."

"Okay, my heart."

"I promise I'll call again."

The next morning, Nadine watched as Ms. Hinds packed her things and changed into a bright-yellow oversized sweatsuit and matching cap while waiting for the doctor to come and sign her discharge papers.

"My mother bought me this hideous outfit," Ms. Hinds wrote on the pad, which was now half filled with words: commands to the nurses, updates to her parents from the previous evening's visit.

"Is someone coming for you?" Nadine asked.

"My parents," Ms. Hinds wrote. Handing Nadine the pad, she reached up and stroked the raised tip of the metal tube in her neck, as if she were worried about her parents seeing it again.

"Good," Nadine said. "The doctor will be here soon."

Nadine was tempted to warn Ms. Hinds that whatever

form of relief she must be feeling now would only last for a while, the dread of being voiceless hitting her anew each day as though it had just happened, when she would awake from dreams in which she'd spoken to find that she had no voice, or when she would see something alarming and realize that she couldn't scream for help, or even when she would realize that she herself was slowly forgetting, without the help of old audio or videocassettes or answering-machine greetings, what her own voice used to sound like. She didn't say anything, however. Like all her other patients, Ms. Hinds would soon find all this out herself.

Nadine spent half her lunch hour staring at the barred windows on the brown building across the alley, watching the Psych nurses scribbling in charts and filing them, rushing to answer sudden calls from the ward.

Josette walked up to the table much earlier than usual, obviously looking for her.

"What is it?" Nadine asked.

"Se Ms. Hinds," Josette said. "She'd like to say good-bye to you."

She thought of asking Josette to tell Ms. Hinds that she couldn't be found, but fearing that this would create some type of conspirational camaraderie between her and Josette, she decided against it.

·   ·   ·

Ms. Hinds and her parents were waiting by the elevator bank in the ward. Ms. Hinds was sitting in a wheelchair with her discharge papers and a clear plastic bag full of odds and ends on her lap. Her father, a strapping man, was clutching the back of the wheelchair with moist, nervous hands, which gripped the chair more tightly for fear of losing hold. The mother, thin and short like Ms. Hinds, looked as though she was fighting back cries, tears, a tempest of anger, barters with God.

Instead she fussed, trying to wrench the discharge papers and the bag from her daughter, irritating Ms. Hinds, who raised her pad from beneath the bag and scribbled quickly, "Nurse Osnac, my parents, Nicole and Justin Hinds."

Nadine shook each parent's hand in turn.

"Glad to make your acquaintance," said the father.

The mother said nothing.

"Thank you for everything," said the father. "Please share our thanks with the doctors, the other nurses, everyone."

The elevator doors suddenly opened and they found themselves staring at the bodies that filled it to capacity, the doctors and nurses traveling between floors, the visitors. The Hindses let the doors close, and the others departed without them.

Ms. Hinds turned to an empty page toward the back of her pad and wrote, "Bye, Nurse Osnac."

"Good luck," Nadine said.

Another elevator opened. There were fewer people in this one and enough room for the Hindses. The father pushed the wheelchair, which jerked forward, nearly dumping Ms. Hinds facefirst into the elevator.

The elevator doors closed behind them sharply, leaving Nadine alone, facing a distorted reflection of herself in the wide, shiny metal surface. Had she carried to full term, her child, aborted two months after his or her conception, would likely have been born today, or yesterday, or tomorrow, probably sometime this week, but this month for certain.

She thought of this for only a moment, then of her parents, of Eric, of the pebble in the water glass in her bedroom at home, all of them belonging to the widened, unrecognizable woman staring back at her from the closed elevator doors.

THE BOOK OF MIRACLES

Anne was talking about miracles right before they reached the cemetery. She was telling her husband and daughter about a case she'd recently heard reported on a religious cable access program, about a twelve-year-old Lebanese girl who cried crystal tears.

From the front passenger seat, the daughter had just blurted out "Ouch!"—one of those non sequiturs that Anne would rather not hear come out of her grown child's mouth but that her daughter sometimes used as a shortcut for more precise reactions to anything that wasn't easily comprehensible. It was either "Ouch!" "Cool," "Okay," or "Whatever," a meaningless litany her daughter had been drawing from since she was fourteen years old.

Anne was thinking of scolding her daughter, of telling her she should talk to them like a woman now, weigh her words carefully so that, even though she was an "artiste," they might take her seriously, but she held back, imagining what her daughter's reaction to her suggestions might be: "Okay, whatever, Manman, please go on with your story."

Her husband, who was always useful in helping her elaborate on her miraculous tales and who also disapproved of their daughter's language, said in Creole, "If crystal was coming out of her eyes, I would think she'd be crying blood."

"That's what's extraordinary," Anne replied. "The crystal pieces were as sharp as knives, but they didn't hurt her."

"How big were these pieces?" the husband asked, slowing the car a bit as they entered the ramp leading to the Jackie Robinson Parkway.

Anne got one last look at the surrounding buildings, which were lit more brightly than usual, with Christmas trees, Chanukah and Kwanzaa candles in most of the windows. She tried to keep these visions in her mind, of illuminated pines, electric candles, and giant cardboard Santas, as the car merged into the curvy, narrow lane. She hated the drive and would have never put herself through it were it not so important to her that her daughter attend Christmas Eve Mass with her and her husband. While in college, her daughter had declared herself an atheist. Between her daughter, who chose not to believe in God, and her husband, who went to the Brooklyn Museum every week, to worship, it seemed to her, at the foot of Ancient Egyptian statues, she felt outnumbered by pagans.

Anne was just about to tell her husband and daughter that the crystal pieces, which had fallen out of the

Lebanese girl's eyes, were as big as ten-carat diamonds—
she imagined her daughter retorting, "I bet her family
wished she cried ten-carat diamonds"— when they reached
the cemetery.

Every time she passed a cemetery, Anne held her
breath. When she was a girl, Anne had gone swimming
with her three-year-old brother on a beach in Grand
Goave, and he had disappeared beneath the waves. Ever
since then, she'd convinced herself that her brother was
walking the earth looking for his grave. Whenever she
went by a cemetery, any cemetery, she imagined him
there, his tiny wet body bent over the tombstones, his
ash-colored eyes surveying the letters, trying to find his
name.

The cemetery was on both sides of them now, the head-
stones glistening in the evening light. She held her breath
the way she imagined her brother did before the weight of
the sea collapsed his small lungs and he was forced to surrender to the water, sinking into a world of starfishes, sea
turtles, weeds, and sharks. She had gone nowhere near the
sea since her brother had disappeared; her heart raced even
when she happened upon images of waves on television.

Who would put a busy thoroughfare in the middle of a
cemetery, she wondered, forcing the living and their noisy
cars to always be trespassing on the dead? It didn't make
sense, but maybe the parkway's architects had been thinking beyond the daily needs of the living. Did they wonder
if the dead might enjoy hearing sounds of life going on at
high speed around them? If this were so, then why should

the living be spared the dead's own signs of existence: of shadows swaying in the breeze, of the laughter and cries of lost children, of the whispers of lovers, muffled as though in dreams.

"We've passed the cemetery," she heard her daughter say.

Anne had closed her eyes without realizing it. Her daughter knew she reacted strongly to cemeteries, but Anne had never told her why, since her daughter had already concluded early in life that this, like many unexplained aspects of her parents' life, was connected to "some event that happened in Haiti."

"I'm glad Papa doesn't have your issues with cemeteries," the daughter was saying, "otherwise we'd be in the cemetery ourselves by now."

The daughter pulled out a cigarette, which the father objected to with the wave of a hand. A former chain-smoker, he could no longer stand the smell of cigarettes.

"When you out the car," he said.

"Yes, sir," the daughter replied, putting the loose cigarette back in its pack. She turned her face to the bare trees lining her side of the parkway and said, "Okay, Manman, please, tell us about another miracle."

A long time ago, more than thirty years ago, in Haiti, your father worked in a prison, where he hurt many people. Now look at him. Look how calm he is. Look how patient he is. Look how he just drove forty miles, to your apartment in Westchester, to pick you up for Christmas Eve Mass. That was the miracle Anne wanted to share with her daughter on this Christmas Eve night, the simple miracle of her husband's transformation, but of course she couldn't, at least not yet, so instead she told of another kind of miracle.

This one concerned a twenty-one-year-old Filipino man who'd seen an image of the Madonna in a white rose petal.

She thought her daughter would dismiss this and just say, "Cool," but instead she actually asked a question. "How come these people are all foreigners?"

"Because Americans don't have much faith," her husband quickly replied, turning his face for a moment to glance at his daughter.

"People here are more practical, maybe," the daughter said, "but there, in Haiti or the Philippines, that's where people see everything, even things they're not supposed to see. So if I see a woman's face in a rose, I'd think somebody drew it there, but if you see it, Manman, you think it's a miracle."

They were coming off the Jackie Robinson Parkway and turning onto Jamaica Avenue, where traffic came to an abrupt stop at the busy intersection. Anne tried to take her mind off the past and bring her thoughts back to the Mass. She loved going to Mass on Christmas Eve, the only time she and her husband and daughter ever attended church together.

When her daughter was a girl, before going to the Christmas Eve Mass, they would drive around their Brooklyn neighborhood to look at the holiday lights. Their community associations were engaged in fierce competition, awarding a prize to the block with the best Nativity scenes, lawn sculptures, wreaths, and banners. Still, Anne and her husband had put up no decorations, fearing, irrationally perhaps, that lit ornaments and trimmings would bring too much attention to them. Instead it was their lack of participation that made them stand out, but by then they had already settled into their routine and couldn't bring themselves to change it.

When her daughter was still living at home, the only way Anne honored the season with her daughter—aside from attending the Christmas Eve Mass—was to put a handful of shredded brown paper under her daughter's bed without her knowledge. The frayed paper was a substitute for the hay that had been part of the baby Jesus' first bed. Over her bedroom doorway, she also hung a sprig of mistletoe. She'd once heard a mistletoe vendor say that mistletoe had all sorts of reconciliatory qualities, so that if two enemies ever found themselves beneath it, they would have to lay down their weapons and embrace each other.

By offering neither each other nor their daughter any presents at Christmas, Anne and her husband had tried to encourage her to be thankful for what she already had—family, a roof over her head—rather than count on what she would, or could, receive on Christmas morning. Their daughter had learned this lesson so well that Christmas no longer interested her. She didn't care about shopping; she didn't watch the endless specials on TV. The only part of the holiday the daughter seemed to enjoy was the drive from block to block to criticize the brightest houses.

"Look at that one," her husband would shout, pointing to the arches of icicle lights draped over one house from top to bottom. "Can you imagine how high their electricity bill is going to be?"

"I wouldn't be able to sleep in a place like that," the daughter would say, singling out a neon holiday greeting in a living room window. "It must be as bright as daylight in there, all the time."

The traffic was flowing again. As they approached St. Thérèse's, her husband and daughter were engaged in their own Christmas ritual, her husband talking about the astronomical cost of Christmas decorations and her daughter saying that one lavishly decorated house after another looked like "an inferno." Meanwhile, Anne tried to think of the Christmas carols they would sing during the Mass. "Silent Night" was her favorite. She hummed the peaceful melody and mouthed the words in anticipation.

Sleep in heavenly peace.
Sleep in heavenly peace.

The church was packed even though the Mass would not begin for another fifteen minutes. Their daughter was outside in the cold, smoking. Anne and her husband found three seats in the next-to-last row, near a young couple who were holding hands and staring ahead at the altar. Anne sat next to the woman, who acknowledged her with a nod as Anne squeezed into the pew.

The daughter soon joined them, plopping herself down on the aisle, next to her father. Anne had tried to convince her to wear a dress, or at least a skirt and a blouse, but she had insisted on wearing her paint-stained blue jeans and a lint-covered sweater.

Anne thought the church most beautiful at Christmas. The Nativity scene in front of the altar had a black Mary, Joseph, and Baby Jesus, the altar candles casting a golden light on their mahogany faces. The sight of people greeting one another around her made her wish that she and her husband had more friends, beyond acquaintances from their respective businesses: the beauty salon and the barbershop. She was beginning to rethink the decision she and her husband had made not to get close to anyone who might ask too many questions about his past. They had set up shop on Nostrand Avenue, at the center of the Haitian community, only because that was where they had the best chance of finding clients. And the only reason they rented the rooms in their basement to three younger Haitian men was because they were the only people who would live there. Besides, soon after her husband had opened his barbershop, he'd discovered that since he'd lost eighty pounds, changed his name, and given as his place of birth a village deep in the mountains of Léogâne, no one asked about him anymore, thinking he was just a peasant who'd made good in New York. He hadn't been a famous "dew breaker," or torturer, anyway, just one of hundreds who had done their jobs so well that their victims were never able to speak of them again.

The church grew silent as the priest walked in and bowed before the altar. It was exactly midnight. Midnight on Christmas Eve was Anne's favorite sixty seconds of the year. It was a charmed minute, not just for her but, she imagined, for the entire world. It was the time when birds were supposed to begin chirping their all-night songs to greet the holy birth, when other animals were to genuflect and trees bow in reverence. She could picture all this as though it were being projected on a giant screen in a movie theater: water in secret wells and far-off rivers and streams was turning into wine; bells were chiming with help only from the breeze; candles, lanterns, and lamps were blinking like the Star of Bethlehem. The gates of Paradise were opened, so anyone who died this minute could enter without passing through Purgatory. The Virgin Mary was choosing among the sleeping children of the world for some to invite to Heaven to serenade her son.

Once again, Anne hoped that the Virgin would choose her young brother to go up to Heaven and sing with the choir of angels. Technically he was not sleeping, but he'd never been buried, so his spirit was somewhere out there, wandering, searching, and if he were chosen to go up to Heaven, maybe the Holy Mother would keep him there.

The priest was incensing the altar, the smoke rising in a perfumed cloud toward the thorn-crowned head on the golden crucifix. Her daughter chose that exact moment to mumble something to her father, while pointing to someone sitting on the aisle, three rows down, diagonally ahead of them.

Anne wanted to tell her daughter to be quiet, but her scolding would mean more conversation, even as her daughter's murmurs were drawing stares from those sitting nearby. When her daughter's garbled whispers grew louder, however, Anne moved her mouth close to her husband's ear to ask, "What?"

"She thinks she sees Emmanuel Constant over there," her husband calmly replied.

It was his turn to point out the man her daughter had been aiming her finger at for a while now. From her limited view of the man's profile, Anne could tell he was relatively tall—even in his seated position his head was visible above those around him—had dark brown skin, a short Afro, a beard. All this was consistent with the picture a community group had printed on the WANTED FOR CRIMES AGAINST THE HAITIAN PEOPLE flyers, which had been stapled to lampposts all along Nostrand Avenue a month before. Beneath the photograph of Constant had been a shorthand list of the crimes of which he had been accused—"torture, rape, murder of 5,000 people"— all apparently committed when he ran a militia ironically called Front for the Advancement and Progress of Haiti.

For a month now, both Anne and her husband had been casting purposefully casual glances at the flyer on the lamppost in front of their stores each morning while opening up and again at night while lowering their shutters. They'd never spoken about the flyer, even when, bleached by the sun and wrinkled by the cold, it slowly began to fade. After a while, the letters and numbers started disappearing so that the word rape became ape and the 5 vanished from 5,000, leaving a trio of zeros as the number of Constant's casualties. The demonic-looking horns that passersby had added to Constant's head and the Creole curses they'd scribbled on the flyer were nearly gone too, turning it into a fragmented collage with as many additions as erasures.

Even before the flyer had found its way to her, Anne had closely followed the story of Emmanuel Constant, through Haitian newspapers, Creole radio and cable access programs. Constant had created his death squad after a military coup had sent Haiti's president into exile. Constant's thousands of disciples had sought to silence the president's followers by circling entire neighborhoods with gasoline, setting houses on fire, and shooting fleeing residents. Anne had read about their campaigns of facial scalping, where skin was removed from dead victims' faces to render them unidentifiable. After the president returned from exile, Constant fled to New York on Christmas Eve. He was tried in absentia in a Haitian court and sentenced to life in prison, a sentence he would probably never serve.

Still, every morning and evening as her eyes wandered to the flyer on the lamppost in front of her beauty salon and her husband's barbershop, Anne had to fight a strong desire to pull it down, not out of sympathy for Constant but out of a fear that even though her husband's prison "work" and Constant's offenses were separated by thirty-plus years, she might arrive at her store one morning to find her husband's likeness on the lamppost rather than Constant's.

"Do you think it's really him?" she whispered to her husband.

He shrugged as someone behind them leaned over and hissed "Shush" into her ear.

The man her daughter believed to be Constant was looking straight ahead. He appeared to be paying close attention as the church choir started a Christmas medley.

> *What child is this, who, laid to rest*
> *On Mary's lap, is sleeping?*

Her daughter was fuming, shifting in her seat and mumbling under her breath, all the while keeping her eyes fixed on the man's profile.

Anne was proud of her daughter, proud of her righteous displeasure. But what if she ever found out about her own father? About the things he had done?

After the sermon, the congregation got up in rows to walk to the front of the church to take Holy Communion.

"How lucky we are," said the priest, "that Jesus was born to give of his flesh for us to take into ourselves."

How lucky *we* are, Anne thought, that we're here at all, that we still have flesh.

When her turn came, Anne got up with a handful of people from her pew, including the young couple sitting next to her, and proceeded to the altar. Uninterested and unconfessed, her husband and daughter remained behind.

Standing before the priest, mouthing the Act of Contrition, she parted her lips to receive the wafer. Then she crossed herself and followed a line of people walking back in the other direction, to their seats.

As she neared the pew where her daughter believed Constant was sitting, she stopped to have a good look at the man on the aisle.

What if it were Constant? What would she do? Would she spit in his face or embrace him, acknowledging a kinship of shame and guilt that she'd inherited by marrying her husband? How would she even know whether Constant felt any guilt or shame? What if he'd come to this Mass to flaunt his freedom? To taunt those who'd been affected by his crimes? What if he didn't even see it that way? What if he considered himself innocent? Innocent enough to go anywhere he pleased? What right did she have to judge him? As a devout Catholic and the wife of a man like her husband, she didn't have the same freedom to condemn as her daughter did.

To get a closer look at the man, she simply lowered her body and moved her face closer to his. She did not even pretend to drop something on the ground, as she'd planned.

Up close, it was instantly obvious that though the man bore a faint resemblance to Constant, it wasn't him. In his most recent pictures, the ones in the newspapers, not the one on the WANTED flyer, Constant appeared much older, fatter, almost twice the size of this man. Constant also had a wider forehead, bushier eyebrows, larger, more bulging eyes, and fuller lips.

Anne straightened her body but still lingered in the aisle, glaring down at the man until he looked up at her and smiled. He seemed to think she was a person he knew too, a face he couldn't immediately place. He looked up expectantly as though waiting for her to say something that would remind him of their connection, but she said nothing. Someone tapped Anne's shoulder from behind and she continued walking, her knees shaking until she got back to her seat.

"Not him," she whispered to her husband.

He turned to his daughter and repeated, "Not him."

While slipping into her seat, Anne whispered these words again to herself. "Not him." It was not him. She felt strangely comforted, as though she, her husband, and her daughter had just been spared bodily harm. Her daughter, however, was still staring at the man doubtfully.

Once everyone who wanted to had received communion, the choir began singing "Silent Night." The tranquility of the melody and the solace of the words were now lost on Anne, for she was thinking that she would never attend this Mass, or any other, with her husband again. What if someone had been sitting there, staring at him, the same way her daughter had been staring at that man? And what if they recognized him, came up to him, and looked into his face?

When the choir finished the song, the priest motioned for them to start again so the congregation could join in.

Anne was surprised to see her husband's lips move as though he were trying to follow along. He missed a few of the verses, lowering his head when he did, but he mostly managed to keep up. She was moved by this gesture, knowing he was singing only because he knew it was her favorite. He was trying to please her, take her mind off the agitation the man's presence had caused her.

During the final blessing, her daughter kept her eyes on the man, craning her neck for a better view of his face.

As soon as the Mass ended, the priest headed down the aisle to greet the congregants on their way out. The people in the front pews followed him. She and her husband and daughter would have to wait until all the rows ahead of them had been emptied before they could exit.

When his turn came, the man they'd believed was Constant strolled past them, chatting with a woman at his side. As he passed her, their daughter raised her hand as if to grab his arm, but her father reached over, lowered it, and held it to her side until the man was beyond her reach.

"I wasn't going to hit him," the daughter said. "I was just going to ask his name."

The daughter turned to her mother, as if to plead for her understanding and said, "Would it be so wrong, Manman, to ask his name?"

. . .

When it was their turn to greet the priest, her daughter and husband quickly slipped by him, leaving Anne to face him alone.

"It's nice to see you, Anne," the priest said. "I thought you were going to bring your family."

"I did, Father," she said.

From the church entrance, she looked out into the street, where most of the congregation had spilled onto the sidewalk. She pushed her head through the doorway until she spotted her husband and daughter crossing the street and moving toward a house with a plastic reindeer on the front lawn.

"There they are, Father," she said, pointing as they reached the white metal fence bordering the house.

The priest turned to look, but couldn't distinguish them from the others spread out now on both sidewalks.

Anne tried to imagine what her husband and daughter could be talking about out there, standing next to that light-drenched fence, their heads nearly touching, as if to shield each other from the cold. Were they discussing the Mass, the man, that house?

"Merry Christmas, Anne," the priest said, trying to move her along. His gaze was already on the person behind her.

"Merry Christmas, Father," Anne said. "It was a lovely Mass."

Stepping outside, Anne joined the crowd on the sidewalk in front of the church, the faces still glowing from the enchantment of the Mass. She didn't rush to cross the street to her husband and daughter, winding her way instead through clusters of families making plans for Christmas dinner, offering and accepting rides, and bundling up their children against the cold.

As she walked the length of the sidewalk, stopping to wish "Merry Christmas" to everyone in her path, she purposely chose families with little boys, stroking their hat-covered heads as she attempted to make small talk with the parents.

"Wasn't it a lovely Mass?"

"Didn't the choir sing well?"

"Papa's ready to go." Her daughter was suddenly at her side, looping her arm through hers. It was a lovely gesture on her daughter's part, her fragile little girl, who'd grown so gruff and distant over the years.

Her husband was still standing across the street. His back was turned to the Christmas house; his hands were buried in his coat pockets, his shoulders hunched against the cold.

"Wasn't it a lovely Mass?" Anne asked her daughter to see whether she was still thinking about the man. If she was, she'd probably say something like, "Yeah, okay, Man-man, it was a fine Mass, until that killer came."

Instead, while waving to her father across the street to show that she'd found Anne, the daughter said, "Listen, Manman. About that guy. I'm sorry I overreacted. Papa thought I was going to hit him or trip him or something. But I wouldn't do anything like that. I don't really know what happened. I wasn't there."

But I was, Anne wanted to say, or almost.

It was always like this, her life a pendulum between forgiveness and regret, but when the anger dissipated she considered it a small miracle, the same way she thought of her emergence from her occasional epileptic seizures as a kind of resurrection.

Her daughter's breath, mixed in with the cold, was forming an icy vapor in the air in front of them. Then, moving her lips close, her daughter pressed them against Anne's cheek until Anne's face felt warm, almost hot.

"I'm sorry to have to say this too, Manman," the daughter added, moving away, smiling. "We come every year, but it's always the same thing. Same choir. Same songs. Same Mass. It was only a Mass. Nothing more. It's never as fabulous as one of your miracles."

NIGHT TALKERS

He thought that the mountain would kill him, that he would never see the other side. He had been walking for two hours when suddenly he felt a sharp pain in his side. He tried some breathing exercises he remembered from medical shows on television, but it was hard to concentrate. All he could think of, besides the pain, was his roommate, Michel, who'd had an emergency appendectomy a few weeks before in New York. What if he was suddenly stricken with appendicitis, here on top of a mountain, deep in the Haitian countryside, where the closest village seemed like a grain of sand in the valley below?

Hugging his midsection, he left the narrow trail and took cover from the scorching midday sun under a tall, arched, wind-deformed tree. Avoiding a row of anthills, he slid down onto his back over a patch of grainy pebbled soil and closed his eyes, shutting out, along with the sapphire sky, the craggy hills that made up the rest of his journey.

He was on his way to visit his aunt Estina, his father's older sister, whom he'd not seen since he moved to New York ten years before. He had lost his parents to the dictatorship twenty-five years before that, when he was a boy, and his aunt Estina had raised him in the capital. After he moved to New York, she returned to her home in the mountains where she'd always taken him during school holidays. This was the first time he was going to her village, as he'd come to think of it, without her. If she had been with him, she would have made him start his journey earlier in the day. They would have boarded a camion at the bus depot in Port-au-Prince before dawn and started climbing the mountain at sunrise to avoid sunstroke at high noon. If she had known he was coming, she would have hired him a mule and sent a child to meet him halfway, a child who would know all the shortcuts to her village. She also would have advised him to wear a sun hat and bring more than the two bottles of water he'd consumed hours ago.

But no, he'd wanted to surprise her; however, the only person he was surprising was himself, by getting lost and nearly passing out and possibly lying there long enough to draw a few mountain vultures to come pick his skeleton clean.

When he finally opened his eyes, the sun was beating down on his face in pretty, symmetrical designs. Filtered through the long, upturned branches of what he now recognized as a giant saguaro cactus, the sun rays had patterned themselves into hearts, starfishes, and circles looped around one another.

He reached over and touched the cactus's thick trunk, which felt like a needle-filled pincushion or a field of dry grass. The roots were close to the soil, a design that his aunt Estina had once told him would allow the plant to collect as much rainwater as possible. Further up along the spine, on the stem, was a tiny cobalt flower. He wanted to pluck it and carry it with him the rest of the way, but his aunt would scold him. Most cactus flowers bloomed only for a few short days, then withered and died. He should let the cactus enjoy its flower for this brief time, his aunt would say.

The pain in his midsection had subsided, so he decided to get up and continue walking. There were many paths to his aunt's house, and seeing the lone saguaro had convinced him that he was on one of them.

He soon found himself entering a village, where a girl was pounding a pestle in a mortar, forming a small crater in the ground beneath the mortar as a group of younger children watched.

The girl stopped her pounding as soon as she saw him, causing the other children to turn their almost identical brown faces toward him.

"Bonjou, cousins," he said, remembering the childhood greeting his aunt had taught him. When he was a boy, in spite of the loss of his parents, he had thought himself part of a massive family, every child his cousin and every adult his aunt or uncle.

"Bonjou," the children replied.

"Ki jan w ye?" the oldest girl added, distinguishing herself. How are you?

"Could I have some water, please?" he said to her, determining that she was indeed the one in charge.

The girl turned her pestle over to the next-oldest child and ran into the limestone house as he dropped his backpack on the ground and collapsed on the front gallery. The ground felt chilly against his bare legs, as though he'd stumbled into a cold stream with his shorts and T-shirt on.

As one of the younger boys ran off behind the house, the other children settled down on the ground next to him, some of them reaching over and stroking his backpack.

The oldest girl came back with a glass in one hand and an earthen jar in the other. He watched as she poured the water, wondering if it, like her, was a mirage fabricated by his intense thirst. When she handed him the water, he drank it faster than it took her to pour him another glass, then another and another, until the earthen jar was clearly empty.

She asked if he wanted more.

"Non," he replied. "Mèsi." Thank you.

The girl went back into the house to put the earthen jar and glass away. The children were staring up at him, too coy to question him and too curious not to stare. When the girl returned, she went back to her spot behind the mortar and pestle and just stood there as though she no longer knew what to do.

An old man carrying a machete and a sisal knapsack walked up to the bamboo gate that separated the road from the house. The young boy who had run off earlier was at his side.

"How are you, konpè?" the old man asked.

"Uncle," he said, "I was dying of thirst until your grand-daughter here gave me some water to drink."

"My granddaughter?" The old man laughed. "She's my daughter. Do you think I look that old?"

Toothless, he did look old, with a grizzly white beard and a face full of folds and creases that seemed to map out every road he had traveled in his life.

The old man reached over and grabbed one of three wooden poles that held up the front of the house. He stood there for a while, saying nothing, catching his breath. After the children had brought him a calabash filled with water—the glass and earthen jar were obviously reserved for strangers—and two chairs for him and the stranger, he lit his pipe, exhaled a fragrant cloud of fresh tobacco, and asked, "Where are you going, my son?"

"I'm going to see my aunt, Estina Estème," he replied. "She lives in Beau Jour."

The old man removed the pipe from his mouth and reached up to scratch his beard.

"Estina Estème? The same Estina Estème from Beau Jour?"

"The same," he said, growing hopeful that he was not too far from his aunt's house.

"You say she is your aunt?"

"She is," he replied. "You know her?"

"Know her?" the old man retorted. "There are no strangers in these mountains. My grandfather Nozial and her grandfather Dorméus were cousins. Who was your father?"

"My father was Maxo Jean Dorméus," he said.

"The one killed with his wife in that fire?" the old man asked. "They only had the one boy. Estina nearly died in that fire too. Only the boy came out whole."

"I am the boy," he said, an egg-sized lump growing in his throat. He hadn't expected to be talking about these things so soon. He had prepared himself for only one conversation about his parents' death, the one he would inevitably have with his aunt.

The children moved a few inches closer to him, their eyes beaming as though they were being treated to a frightening folktale in the middle of the day.

"Even after all these years," the old man said, "I'm still so sad for you. So you are that young man who used to come here with Estina, the one who went to New York some years back?"

The old man looked him up and down, as if searching for burn marks on his body, then ordered the children to retreat.

"Shoo," he commanded. "This is no talk for young ears."

The children quickly vanished, the oldest girl resuming her work with the mortar and pestle.

Rising from his chair, the old man said, "Come, I'll take you to Estina Estème."

Estina Estème lived in a valley between two lime-green mountains and a giant waterfall, which sprayed a fine mist over the banana grove that surrounded her one-room house and the teal ten-place mausoleum that harbored the bones of many of her forebears. Her nephew recognized the house as soon as he saw it. It had not changed much, the sloped tin roof and the wooden frame intact. His aunt's banana grove seemed to have flourished; it was greener and denser than he remembered. Her garden was packed with orange and avocado trees—a miracle, given the barren mountain range he'd just traveled through.

When he entered his aunt's yard, he was greeted by a flock of hens and roosters that scattered quickly, seeking shelter on top of the family mausoleum.

He rushed to the front porch, where an old faded skirt and blouse were drying on the wooden railing. The door was open, so he ran into the house, leaving behind the old man and a group of neighbors whom the old man had enticed into following them by announcing as he passed their houses that he had with him Estina Estème's only nephew.

In the small room was his aunt's cot, covered with a pale blue sheet. Nearby was a calabash filled with water, within easy reach so she could drink from it at night without leaving her bed. Under the cot was her porcelain chamber pot and baskets filled with a few Sunday dresses, hats, and shoes.

The old man peeked in to ask, "She's not here?"

"No," he replied, "she's not."

He was growing annoyed with the old man, even though he would never have found his aunt's house so quickly without his help.

When he walked out of the house, he found himself facing a dozen or so more people gathered in his aunt's yard. He scanned the faces and recognized one or two, but couldn't recall the names. Many in the group were nudging one another, whispering while pointing at him. Others called out, "Dany, don't you know me anymore?"

He walked over and kissed the women, shook hands with the men, and patted the children's heads.

"Please, where's my aunt?" he asked of the entire crowd.

"She'll soon be here," a woman replied. "We sent for her."

Once he knew his aunt was on her way, he did his best to appear interested in catching up. Many in the crowd complained that once he got to New York, he forgot about them, never sending the watch or necklace or radio he'd promised. Surprised that they'd taken his youthful pledges so seriously, he offered some feeble excuses. "It's not so easy to earn money in New York. . . . I thought you'd moved to the capital. . . . I didn't know your address."

"Where would we have gone?" one of the men rebutted. "We were not so lucky as you."

He was glad when he heard his aunt's voice, calling his name. The crowd parted and she appeared, pudgy yet graceful in a drop-waist dress. Her face was round and full, her skin silken and very black, her few wrinkles, in his estimation, more like beauty marks than signs of old age. Two people were guiding her by the elbows. As they were leading her to him, she pulled herself away and raised her hands in front of her, searching for him in the breeze. He had almost forgotten that she was blind, had been since the day of the fire that had taken his parents' lives.

The crowd moved back a few feet as he ran into her arms. She held him tightly, angling her head to kiss the side of his face.

"Dany, is it you?" She patted his back and shoulders to make sure.

"I brought him here for you," the old man said.

"Old Zo, why is it that you're always mixed up in everything?" she asked, joking.

"True to my name," the old man replied, "I'm a bone that fits every stew."

The crowd laughed.

"Let's go in the house," his aunt told him. "It's hot out here."

As they started for her front door, he took her hand and tried to guide her, but found himself an obstacle in her path and let go. Once they were inside, she felt her way to her cot and sat down on the edge.

"Sit with me, Da," she said. "You have made your old aunt a young woman again."

"How are you?" He sat down next to her. "Truly?"

"*Truly* fine," she said. "Did Popo tell you different?"

For years now, he'd been paying a boyhood friend in Port-au-Prince, Popo, to come and check on her once a month. He would send Popo money to buy her whatever she needed and Popo would in turn call him in New York to brief him on how she was doing.

"No," he said. "Popo didn't tell me anything."

"Then why did you come?" she asked. "I'm not unhappy to see you, but you just dropped out of the sky. There must be a reason." She felt for his face, found it, and kissed it for what seemed like the hundredth time. "Were you sent back?" she asked. "We have a few boys here in the village who have been sent back. Many don't even speak Creole anymore. They come here because this is the only place they have any family. There's one boy not far from here. I'll take you to visit him. You can speak to him, one American to another."

"You still go on your visits?" he asked.

"When they came to fetch me, I was with a girl in labor," she said.

"Still midwifing?"

"Helping the midwife," she replied. "You know I know every corner of these mountains. If a new tree grows, I learn where it is. Same with children. A baby's still born the same way it was when I had sight."

"I meant to come sooner," he said, watching her join and separate her fingers like tree branches brushing against each other. Both her hands had been burned during the fire that had followed the explosion at his parents' house, but over the years the burn marks had smoothed into her skin and were now barely visible.

"I knew that once the time was right you'd come back," she said. "But why didn't you send word that you were on your way?"

"You're right," he said. "I didn't just drop out of the sky. I came because I want to tell you something."

"What is it, Da?" she asked, weaving and unweaving her fingers. "Are you finally getting married?"

"No," he said. "That's not it. I found him. I found him in New York, the man who killed Papa and Manman and took your sight."

Why the old man chose that exact moment to come through the door he would never know. Perhaps it was chance, serendipity, or maybe simply because the old man was a nosy pain in the ass. But just then Old Zo came in, pushing the mortar-and-pestle girl ahead of him. She was carrying a covered plate of food.

"We brought you something to refresh you," he told Dany.

His aunt seemed neither distressed nor irritated by the interruption. She could have sent Old Zo and the girl away, but she didn't. Instead she told them to put their offering on an old table in the corner. The girl quietly put the plate down and backed out of the room, avoiding Dany's eyes.

"I hope you're both hungry," the old man said, not moving from his spot. "Everyone is going to bring you something."

Clusters of food-bearing people streamed in and out of the house all afternoon. He and his aunt would sample each plate, then share the rest with the next visitor until everyone in the valley had tasted at least one of their neighbors' dishes.

By the time all the visitors had left and he and his aunt were alone together, it was dark and his aunt showed no interest in hearing what he had to say. Instead she offered him her cot, but he talked her into letting him have the sisal mat she'd spread out on the floor for herself.

She fell asleep much more quickly than he did. Mid-dream, she laughed, paid compliments, made promises, or gave warnings. "Listen, don't go too far. Come back soon. What a strong baby! I'll make you a dress. I'll make you coffee." Then she sat up in her cot to scold herself, "Estina, you are waking the boy," before drifting once again into the images in her head.

In the dark, listening to his aunt conduct entire conversations in her sleep, he realized that aside from blood, she and he shared nocturnal habits. They were both palannits, night talkers, people who wet their beds, not with urine but with words. He too spoke his dreams aloud in the night, to the point of sometimes jolting himself awake with the sound of his own voice. Usually he could remember only the very last words he spoke, but remained with a lingering sensation that he had been talking, laughing, and at times crying all night long.

His aunt was already awake by the time he got up the next morning. With help from Old Zo's daughter, who seemed to have been rented out to his aunt for the duration of his visit, she had already set up breakfast on the small table brought out to the front gallery from inside the house. His aunt seemed restless, almost anxious, as if she'd been waiting for him to rise for hours.

"Go wash yourself, Da," she said, handing him a towel. "I'll be waiting for you here."

Low shrubs covered in dew brushed against his ankles as he made his way down a trail toward the stream at the bottom of the fall. The water was freezing cold when he slipped in, but he welcomed the sensation of having almost every muscle in his body contract, as if to salute the dawn.

Had his father ever bathed in this stream? Had his parents soaked here together, in this same spot, when they'd come to stay with his aunt? He had so little information and so few memories to draw on that every once in a while he would substitute moments from his own life in trying to re-create theirs. But lately what was taking up the most space in his mind was not the way his parents had lived but the way they had died.

A group of women were coming down the path toward

the river with calabashes and plastic jugs balancing on top
of their heads. They would bathe, then fill their containers
further up, closer to the fall. He remembered spending
hours as a boy watching the women bathe topless, their
breasts flapping against their chests as they soaped and
scrubbed themselves with mint and parsley sprigs, as if to
eradicate every speck of night dust from their skin.

When he got back to his aunt's house, he had a visitor, a
short, muscular boy with a restrained smile and an overly
firm handshake. The boy's brawny arms were covered
with tattoos from his elbows down to his wrists, his skin a
canvas of Chinese characters, plus kings and queens from
a card deck. One-Eyed Jack, Hector, Lancelot, Judith,
Rachel, Argine, and Palas, they were all there in miniature,
carved into his nut-brown skin in navy blue and red ink.

"I sent for Claude," his aunt announced. "He's the one
I was telling you about, one of the boys who was sent
back."

Claude was sitting next to his aunt, on the top step in
front of the house, dipping his bread in the coffee Old
Zo's daughter had just made.

"Claude understands Creole and is learning to speak bit
by bit," his aunt said, "but he has no one to speak English
to. I would like you to talk with him."

Claude was probably in his late teens, too young, it
seemed, to have been expatriated twice, from both his
native country and his adopted land. Dany sat down on
the step next to Claude, and Old Zo's daughter handed
him a cup of coffee and a piece of bread.

"How long have you been here?" he asked Claude.

"Too long, man," Claude replied, "but I guess it could be worse. I could be down in the city, in Port, eating crap and sleeping on the street. Everyone here's been really cool to me, especially your aunt. She's really taken me under her wing."

Claude flapped his heavily tattooed arms, as if to illustrate the word "wing."

"When I first got here," he continued, "I thought I'd get stoned. I mean, I thought people would throw rocks at me, man. Not the other kind of stoned. I mean, coming out of New York, then being in prison in Port for three months because I had no place to go, then finally my moms, who didn't speak to me for the whole time I was locked up, came to Port and hooked me up with some family up here."

His aunt was leaning forward with both hands holding up her face, her white hair braided like a crown of gardenias around her head. She was listening to them speak, like someone trying to capture the indefinable essence of a great piece of music. Watching her face, the pleasure she was taking in the unfamiliar words made him want to talk even more, find something drawn-out to say, tell a story of some kind, even recite some poetry, if only he knew any.

"So you're getting by all right?" he asked Claude.

"It took a lot of getting used to, but I'm settling in," Claude replied. "I got a roof over my head and it's quiet as hell here. No trouble worth a damn to get into. It's cool that you've come back to see your aunt, man. Some of the folks around here told me she had someone back in New York. I had a feeling when she'd ask me to speak English for her."

Claude reached down and picked up a couple of pebbles from the ground. It seemed to Dany that he could easily crush them if he wanted to, pulverize them with his fingertips. But instead he took turns throwing them up in the air and catching them, like a one-handed juggler. "It's real big that you didn't forget her, that you didn't forget your folks," he went on. "I wish I'd stayed in touch more with my people, you know; then it wouldn't be so weird showing up here like I did. These people don't even know me, man. They've never seen my face before, not even in pictures. They still took me in, after everything I did, because my moms told them I was their blood. I look at them and I see nothing of me, man, blank, nada, but they look at me and they say he has so-and-so's nose and his grandmother's forehead, or some shit like that." One of Claude's pebbles fell on the ground, missing his hand. He did not bend down to pick it up, but threw the others after it. "It's like a puzzle, a weird-ass kind of puzzle, man," he said. "I'm the puzzle and these people are putting me back together, telling me things about myself and my family that I never knew or gave a fuck about. Man, if I'd run into these people back in Brooklyn, I'd have laughed my ass off at them. I would've called them backward-ass peasants. But here I am."

His aunt was engrossed, enthralled by Claude's speech, smiling at times while the morning rays danced across her eyes, never penetrating her pupils. He was starting to think of his aunt's eyes as a strange kind of prism, one that consumed light rather than reflected it.

"I can't honestly say I love it here," Claude seemed to be wrapping up, "but it's worked out good for me. It saved my life. I'm at peace here, and my family seems to have made peace with me. I came around; I can honestly say I was reformed in prison. I would've been a better citizen than most if they hadn't deported me."

"You still have a chance," Dany said, not believing it himself. "You can do something with your life. Maybe you're back here for a reason, to make things better."

He was growing tired of Claude, tired of what he considered his lame excuses and an apparent lack of remorse for whatever it was he'd done.

"How long will you be staying?" Claude asked.

"A while," Dany said.

"Is there anything you want to do?" Claude asked. "I know the area pretty well now. I take lots of walks to clear my head. I could show you around."

"I know where things are," Dany said. "And if I don't remember, my aunt can—"

"It's just with her not being able to see—"

"She can see, in her own way."

"Cool, man. I was just trying to be helpful."

Even with the brusque way their conversation ended, Claude seemed happy as he left. He had gotten his chance to speak English and tell his entire life story in the process.

After Claude's departure, Old Zo's daughter came up

and took the empty coffee cup from Dany's hand. She lingered in front of him for a minute, her palm accidentally brushing against his fingertips. At times, she seemed older than she looked. Maybe she was twenty, twenty-five, but she looked twelve. He wondered what her story was. Were those children he had seen in Old Zo's yard hers? Did she have a husband? Was he in the city? Dead?

She hesitated before stepping away, as though she gave too much thought to every move she made. When she finally walked away, Dany's aunt asked him, "Do you know why Claude was in prison?"

"He didn't say."

"Do you know what his people say?"

"What do his people say?"

"They say he killed his father."

That night, Dany dreamed that he was having the conversation he'd come to have with his aunt. They were sitting on the step where he and Claude had spoken. He began the conversation by recalling with his aunt the day his parents died.

He was six years old and his father was working as a gardener in Port-au-Prince. The night of the explosion, he had been at home with his parents and his aunt, who was visiting from Beau Jour, when they heard a loud crash outside. His father went out first, followed by his mother. Dany was about to go after them when he heard the shots.

His aunt grabbed him and pinned him to the ground, but somehow he managed to wiggle out of her grasp.

Outside, most of the wooden porch was already on fire. The smoke was so dense he could barely see his parents, his mother slumped over his father on the ground.

Behind him the front door was covered in flames. He ran out to the yard and called out for his aunt at the top of his lungs.

"Shut up now or I'll shoot you too!" someone was shouting from the street.

It was a large man with a face like a soccer ball and a widow's peak dipping into the middle of his forehead. The man was waving a gun at him as he opened his car door, and he only lowered the gun to drive away. His aunt then crawled out of the house and away from the porch, coughing the smoke out of her lungs. She was unable to see.

He dreamed his aunt saying, "Yes, this is how it happened, Da," then urging him to elaborate on what he'd begun to tell her before Old Zo and his daughter had walked into her house. "You said you saw that same man in New York, Da? Are you sure it was him?"

The man who had killed his parents was now a barber in New York. He had a wife and a grown daughter, who visited often. Some guys from work had told him that a barber was renting a room in the basement of his house. When he went to the barbershop to ask about the room, he recognized the barber as the man who had waved the gun at him outside his parents' house.

"It's been so many years," the dream aunt said. "Are you sure he's the one?"

He took the empty room in the barber's basement. He couldn't sleep for months, spending his weekends in nightclubs to pass the time. He visited the barbershop regularly for haircuts, arriving early in the morning soon after he opened. He would sit and watch the barber, now a much thinner man, turn on his radio, then sweep the entire shop before lining up his tools and calling him to the chair. His heart would race as the barber draped a black cape over his chest, then sheared paths through his hair until barely a stubble was left on top of his head. All the while he would study the pictures on the walls, campaign posters for local elections, hairstyle samples that he never chose from, asking the barber only to "cut as much as you can."

The barber never made conversation, never said, "How do you like the basement?" He only asked in a soft voice that sounded nothing like the hoarse and angry voice that had threatened him so many years ago, "Would you like a shave?"

He never turned down the shaves, for he thought it would give the barber a chance to have a closer look at his face, to remember him. He always expected the barber's large hands to tremble, but it was his own body that quivered instead, his forehead and neck that became covered with sweat, melting the shaving cream on his chin, forcing the barber to offer him extra napkins and towels and warn him to stay still to avoid nicks and cuts.

Finally, two nights ago, when the barber's wife was away at a religious retreat—he looked for such opportunities all the time and hadn't found one until then—he climbed the splintered steps to the first floor, then made his way with a flashlight to the barber's bedroom.

"What did you do?" the dream aunt asked.

He stood there and listened to the barber breathing. The barber was snoring, each round of snores beginning with a grunt and ending in a high-pitched moan. He lowered his face toward the barber's widow's peak, hoping he would wake him up and startle him to death. When he was a boy, he'd heard about political prisoners being choked in their sleep, their faces swelling, their eyes bulging out of their heads. He wanted to do the same thing now to the barber. Or maybe press a pillow down on his face. Or simply wake him up to ask him "Why?"

Looking down at the barber's face, which had shrunk so much over the years, he lost the desire to kill. It wasn't that he was afraid, for he was momentarily feeling bold, fearless. It wasn't pity, either. He was too angry to feel pity. It was something else, something less measurable. It was the dread of being wrong, of harming the wrong man, of making the wrong woman a widow and the wrong child an orphan. It was the realization that he would never know why—why one single person had been given the power to destroy his entire life.

He was trembling again. His whole body, it seemed, was soaked with sweat as he tiptoed out of the barber's room. Even when he was back in the basement calling about flights to Port-au-Prince, he couldn't shake the feeling that after all these years the barber might finally make good on his promise to shoot him, just as he had his parents.

Dany woke himself with the sound of his own voice reciting his story. His aunt was awake too; he could make out her outline in the dark. It looked as though she was sitting up in her cot, pushing the chamber pot beneath her, to relieve herself.

"Da, were you dreaming about your parents?" She leaned over and replaced the chamber pot back under the bed. "You were calling their names."

"Was I?" He would have thought he was calling the barber.

"You were calling your parents," she said, "just this instant."

He was still back there, on the burning porch, hoping that his mother and father would rise and put out the fire. He was in the yard, watching the barber's car speed away and his aunt crawling off the porch, on her belly, like a blind snake. He was in that room in Brooklyn, with the barber, watching him sleep. Now his aunt's voice was just an echo of things he could no longer enjoy—his mother's voice, his father's laugh.

"I'm sorry I woke you," he said, wiping the sweat off his forehead with the backs of his hands.

"I should have let you continue telling me what you came here to say." His aunt's voice seemed to be floating toward him in the dark. "It's like walking up these mountains and losing something precious halfway. For you, it would be no problem walking back to find it because you're still young and strong, but for me it would take a lot more time and effort."

He heard the cot squeak as she lay back down.

"Tante Estina," he said, lying back on the small sisal mat himself.

"Wi, Da," she replied.

"Were my parents in politics?"

"Oh, Da," she said, as if protesting the question.

"Please," he said.

"No more than any of us," she said.

"What do you mean?" he asked.

"They didn't do anything bad, Da," she said, "or anything at all. I didn't know all my brother's secrets, but I think he was taken for somebody else."

"Who?" he asked.

"M pa konnen," she said.

He thought maybe she'd said a name, Lubin or Firmin.

"Who were they mistaken for?" he asked her again.

"M pa konnen," she repeated. "I don't know, Da. Maybe they were mistaken for all of us. There's a belief that if you kill people, you can take their knowledge, become everything they were. Maybe they wanted to take all that knowledge for themselves. I don't know, Da. All I know is I'm very tired now. Let me sleep."

He decided to let her rest. They should have a chance to talk again. She went back to sleep, whispering some-

thing he could not hear under her breath, then growing silent. When he woke up the next morning, she was
dead.

It was Old Zo's daughter who let out the first cry,
announcing the death to the entire valley. Sitting near the
body, on the edge of his aunt's cot, Dany was doubled
over with an intense bellyache. Old Zo's daughter took
over immediately, brewing him some tea while waiting for
their neighbors to arrive.

The tea did nothing for him. He wasn't expecting it to.
Part of him was grateful for the pain, for the physically
agonizing diversion it provided him.

Soon after Old Zo's daughter's cry, a few of the village
women started to arrive. It was only then that he learned
Old Zo's daughter's name, at least her nickname, Ti Fanm,
Little Woman, which the others kept shouting as they
badgered her with questions.

"What happened, Ti Fanm?"

"Ti Fanm, did she die in her sleep?"

"Did she fall, Ti Fanm?"

"Ti Fanm, did she suffer?"

"Ti Fanm, she wasn't even sick."

"She was old," Ti Fanm said in a firm and mature voice.
"It can happen like that."

They didn't bother asking him anything. He wouldn't
have known how to answer anyway. After he and his aunt
had spoken in the middle of the night, he thought she had

fallen asleep. When he woke up in the morning, even later than he had the day before, she was still lying there, her eyes shut, her hands resting on her belly, her fingers intertwined. He tried to find her pulse, but she had none. He lowered his face to her nose and felt no breath; then he walked out of the house and found Ti Fanm, sitting on the steps, waiting to cook their breakfast. The pain was already starting in his stomach. Ti Fanm came in and performed her own investigation on his aunt, then let out that cry, a cry as loud as any siren he had heard on the streets of New York.

His aunt's house was filled with people now, each of them taking turns examining his aunt's body for signs of life, and when finding none immediately assigning themselves, and one another, tasks related to her burial. One group ran off to get purple curtains, to hang shroudlike over the front door to show that this was a household in mourning. Another group went off to fetch an unused washbasin to bathe the corpse. Others were searching through the baskets beneath his aunt's cot for an appropriate dress to change her into after her bath. Another went looking for a carpenter to build her coffin.

The men assigned themselves to him and his pain.

"He's in shock," they said.

"Can't you see he's not able to speak?"

"He's not even looking at her. He's looking at the floor."

"He has a stomachache," Ti Fanm intercepted.

She brought him some salted coffee, which he drank in one gulp.

"He should lie down," one of the men said.

"But where?" another rebutted. "Not next to her."

"He must have known she was going to die." He heard Old Zo's voice rising above the others. "He came just in time. Blood calls blood. She made him come so he could see her before she died. It would have been sad if she'd died behind his back, especially given the way he lost his parents."

They were speaking about him as though he couldn't understand, as if he were solely an English speaker, like Claude. He wished that his stomach would stop hurting, that he could rise from the edge of the cot and take control of the situation, or at least participate in the preparations, but all he wanted to do was lie down next to his aunt, rest his head on her chest, and wrap his arms around her waist, the way he had done when he was a boy. He wanted to close his eyes until he could wake up from this unusual dream where everyone was able to speak except the two of them.

By midday, he felt well enough to join Old Zo and some of the men who were opening an empty slot in the family mausoleum. He was in less pain now, but was still uncomfortable and moved slower than the others.

Old Zo announced that a Protestant minister would be coming by the next morning to say a prayer during the burial. Old Zo had wanted to transport the body to a church in the next village for a full service, but Dany was sure that his aunt wouldn't have wanted to travel so far, only to return to her own yard to be buried.

"I've been told that the coffin's almost ready," Old Zo said. "She'll be able to rest in it during the wake."

Ti Fanm and the other women were inside the house, bathing his aunt's body and changing her into a blue dress he'd sent her last Christmas through Popo. He had seen the dress in a store window on Nostrand Avenue and had chosen it for her, remembering that blue was her favorite color. The wrapping was still intact; she had never worn it.

Before he left the room he watched as Ti Fanm handed a pair of rusty scissors along with the dress to one of the oldest women, who proceeded to clip three small pieces from the inner lining. As the old woman "marked" the dress, the others moaned, some whispering and some shouting, "Estina, this is your final dress. Don't let anyone take it from you. Even if among the other dead there are some who are naked, this is your dress and yours alone. Don't give it away."

He'd heard his aunt talk about this ritual, this branding of the final clothes, but had never seen it done before. His parents' clothes had not been marked because they had been secretly and hastily buried. Now in his pocket he had three tiny pieces of cloth that had been removed from the lining of his aunt's last dress, and he would carry them with him forever, like some people carry locks of hair or fingernails.

·   ·   ·

He had always been perplexed by the mixture of jubilation and sorrow that was part of Beau Jour's wakes, by the fact that some of the participants played cards and dominoes while others served tea and wept. But what he most enjoyed was the time carved out for the mourners to tell stories about the deceased, singular tales of first or last encounters, which could make one either chuckle or weep.

The people of his aunt's village were telling such stories about her now. They told of how she had once tried to make coffee and filtered dirt through her coffee pouch, how she had once delivered the village's only triplets, saving all three babies and the mother.

"In the city that kind of birthing might have required a serious operation," Old Zo said, "but we didn't need the city doctors. Estina knew what to do."

"Here's one she brought into the world," a man said, pushing a boy forward.

"Here's another," someone else said.

"She birthed me," a young man said. "Since my mother died, she's been like a mother to me, because she was the only other person present at my birth."

They told of how as a young woman his aunt had embroidered a trousseau that she carried everywhere with her, thinking it would attract a husband. They spoke of her ambition, of her wanting to be a baby seamstress, so she could make clothes for the very same children she was ushering into the world. If he could have managed it, he would have told her neighbors how she had treated her burns herself after the fire, with poultices and herbs. He'd have spoken of her sacrifices, of the fact that she had spent most of her life trying to keep him safe. He would have told of how he hadn't wanted to leave her, to go to New York, but she'd insisted that he go so he would be as far away as possible from the people who'd murdered his parents.

Claude arrived at the wake just as it was winding down, at a time when everyone was too tired to do anything but sit, stare, and moan, when through sleepy eyes the reason for the all-night gathering had become all too clear, when the purple shroud blowing from the doorway into the night breeze could no longer be ignored.

"I'm sorry, man," Claude said. "Your aunt was such good people. One of a kind. I'm truly sorry."

Claude moved forward, as if to hug Dany, his broad shoulders towering over Dany's head. Dany stepped back, cringing. Maybe it was what his aunt had told him, about Claude having killed his father, but he didn't want Claude to touch him.

Claude got the message and walked away, drifting toward a group of men who were nodding off at a table near the porch railing.

When he walked back inside the house, Dany found a few women sitting near the plain pine coffin, keeping watch over his aunt. He was still unable to look at her in the coffin for too long. He envied these women the ten years they'd spent with her while he was gone. He dragged his sisal mat, the one he'd been sleeping on these last two nights, to a corner, one as far away from the coffin as possible.

It could happen like that, Ti Fanm had said. A person his aunt's age could fall asleep talking and wake up dead. He wouldn't have believed it if he hadn't seen it for himself. Death was supposed to be either quick and furious or drawn out and dull, after a long illness. Maybe Old Zo was right. Blood calls blood. Perhaps she had summoned him here so he could at last witness a peaceful death and see how it was meant to be mourned. Perhaps the barber was not his parents' murderer after all, but just a phantom who'd shown up to escort him back here.

He could not fall asleep, not with the women keeping watch over his aunt's body being so close by. Not with Ti Fanm coming over every hour with a cup of tea, which was supposed to cure his bellyaches forever.

He didn't like her nickname, was uncomfortable using it. It felt too generic to him, as though she were one of many from a single mold, with no distinctive traits of her own.

"What's your name?" he asked when she brought him her latest brew.

She seemed baffled, as though she were thinking he might need a stronger infusion, something to calm his nerves and a memory aid too.

"Ti Fanm," she replied.

"Non," he said. "Your true name, your full name."

"Denise Auguste," she said.

The women who were keeping watch over his aunt were listening to their conversation, cocking their heads ever so slightly in their direction.

"How old are you?" he asked.

"Twenty," she said.

"Thank you," he said.

"You're deserving," she said, using an old-fashioned way of acknowledging his gratitude.

She was no longer avoiding his eyes, as though his grief and stomach ailment and the fact that he'd asked her real name had rendered them equals.

He got up and walked outside, where many of his aunt's neighbors were sleeping on mats on the porch. There was a full moon overhead and a calm in the air that he was not expecting. In the distance, he could hear the waterfall, a sound that, once you got used to it, you never paid much attention to. He walked over to the mausoleum, removed his shirt, and began to wipe it, starting at the base and working his way up toward the flat top surface and the cross. It was clean already. The men had done a good job removing the leaves, pebbles, and dust that had accumulated on it while they were opening his aunt's slot, but he wanted to make sure it was spotless, that every piece of debris that had fallen on it since was gone.

"Need help?" Claude asked from a few feet away.

He'd been sitting on the porch with some of the men.

Dany threw his dusty shirt on the ground, climbed on top of the mausoleum, and sat down. His aunt's body would be placed in one of the higher slots, one of two not yet taken.

"Excuse me," Dany said, "for earlier."

"I understand," Claude said. "I'd be a real asshole if I got pissed off at you for anything you did or said to me at a time like this. You're in pain, man. I get that."

"I don't know if I'd call it pain," Dany said. "There's no word yet for it. No one has thought of a word yet."

"I know, man," Claude said. "It's a real bitch."

In spite of his huge muscles and oversized tattoos, Claude seemed oddly defenseless, like a refugee lost at sea, or a child looking for his parents in a supermarket aisle. Or maybe that's just how Dany wanted to see him, to make him seem more normal, less frightening.

"I hear you killed your father," Dany said.

The words sounded less severe coming out of his mouth than they did rolling around in his head. Claude pushed both his hands into his pants pockets and looked off into the distance toward the banana groves.

"Can I sit?" he asked, turning his face back toward the mausoleum platform, where Dany was sitting.

"I didn't mean to say it like that," Dany said. "It's not my business."

"Yes, I killed my old man," Claude said in the same abrupt tone that he used for everything else. "Everyone here knows that by now. I wish I could say it was an accident. I wish I could say he was a bastard who beat the crap out of me and forced me to defend myself. I wish I could tell you I hated him, never loved him, didn't give a fuck about him at all. I was fourteen and strung out on shit. He came into my room and took the shit. It wasn't just my shit. It was shit I was hustling for someone else. I was really fucked up and wanted the shit back. I had a gun I was using to protect myself out on the street. I threatened him with it. He wouldn't give my shit back, so I shot him."

There was even less sorrow in Claude's voice than Dany had expected. Perhaps Claude too had never learned how to grieve or help others grieve. Maybe the death of a parent early in life, either by one's own hand or by others, eliminated that instinct in a person.

"I'm sorry," Dany said, feeling that someone should also think of a better word for their particular type of sorrow.

"Sorry?" Claude wiped a shadow of a tear from his face with a quick swipe of the back of his hand. "I'm the luckiest fucker alive. I've done something really bad that makes me want to live my life like a fucking angel now. If I hadn't been a minor, I'd have been locked up for the rest of my life. They might have even given me the chair. And if the prisons in Port had had more room, or if the police down there were worth a damn, I'd be in a small cell with a thousand people right now, not sitting here talking to you."

Claude threw his hands up in the air and, raising his voice, as if to call out to the stars slowly evaporating from the sky, shouted, "Even with everything I've done, with everything that's happened to me, I'm the luckiest fucker on this goddamned planet. Someone somewhere must be looking out for my ass."

It would be an hour or so now before Dany's aunt's burial at dawn. The moon was already fading, slipping away, on its way to someplace else. The only thing Dany could think to do for his aunt now was to keep Claude speaking, which wouldn't be so hard, since Claude was already one of them, a member of their tribe. Claude was a palannit, a night talker, one of those who spoke their nightmares out loud to themselves. Except Claude was even luckier than he realized, for he was able to speak his nightmares to himself as well as to others, in the nighttime as well as in the hours past dawn, when the moon had completely vanished from the sky.

THE BRIDAL SEAMSTRESS

Beatrice Saint Fort was lying down for one of her mid-day siestas when a journalism intern arrived at her new house in Far Rockaway, Queens, to interview her for a short feature on her last day as a bridal seamstress. The intern, a striking Haitian American girl with waist-length, amber-hued dreadlocks and a gold loop in her right nostril, had to knock several times before Beatrice finally made it to the front door in a green flannel nightgown and matching rabbit-shaped slippers. Beatrice held the door half open, rubbing the sleep out of her eyes, while barring the entrance with her wispy frame. A petite, wasp-waisted woman, Beatrice had shoulders that curved, and she bent forward as though she'd spent too much time searching for things on the ground.

"My name is Aline Cajuste," the intern said. "I called yesterday and you told me to come at two?"

"Oh," Beatrice said, running her long, veined fingers over the rainbow cap that covered her bullet-shaped head.

"May I come in?" Aline asked.

"Sure," Beatrice said. In spite of her size she had a loud, commanding voice, like someone who was accustomed to giving orders. "Have a seat while I get myself ready."

A half hour later, a more youthful-looking and made-up Beatrice emerged, wearing a purple tunic dress and a curly bronze wig pinned to her scalp. Putting aside a profile of the actress Gabrielle Fonteneau that she was reading from her own newspaper ("A model of the kind of uplifting articles you should attempt," her editor in chief, Marjorie Voltaire, had said), Aline looked up from the plastic-covered couch near the window where she'd sat since Beatrice had disappeared and politely asked, "May we begin?"

"Sure," Beatrice said, "but first let me make you some coffee."

Before Aline could refuse the coffee, Beatrice vanished behind the louvered door separating the living room from the rest of the house, giving Aline another chance to look around and jot down a few notes.

The living room was bare enough to make setting up the piece an easy task. Aside from some taped boxes piled in a corner, there were only the couch and a glass coffee table. On the wall was a picture of Jesus, neither white nor black, but somewhere in between, and beneath it a headless dressmaker's model covered with a beaded lace gown.

"Can I help?" Aline called from the living room.

"Don't move," Beatrice called back. "I won't be long!"

By Aline's watch, it took Beatrice another twenty minutes to make the coffee. When Beatrice finally resurfaced, Aline promised herself she wouldn't let the woman out of her sight again until they'd completed the interview.

"Okay." Beatrice sat down on the couch, watching Aline. "Tell me, is this the best coffee you've ever had?"

Indeed it was. Aline had an expensive espresso machine at home that she'd not yet gotten to produce anything nearly as delicious as Beatrice's coffee. The espresso machine was a college graduation gift from her thirty-years-older girlfriend; she'd shipped it to Aline all the way from Miami, where she'd gotten a new chaired position in the psychology department at Florida International. On a late-night call, during finals week, she'd asked Aline what she wanted most after graduation, and still exhausted from back-to-back all-nighters, Aline had mumbled that she wanted (1) to stop drinking watered-down coffee, (2) to eat no more frozen dinners, and (3) to do something with her life.

She'd sent Aline the espresso maker and a three-hundred-dollar gift certificate for a five-star restaurant meal. "The rest," she'd written on her newly monogrammed stationery card, "you have to figure out yourself."

Beatrice's coffee was beginning to relax Aline. Ignoring her editor's advice ("Don't get too cozy with the natives," she'd told Aline soon after she'd offered her the internship), Aline was tasting spirits in the coffee, but couldn't identify which. Beatrice had brewed the coffee in a way that overpowered whatever she'd added to it, but still left its effects intact.

The tips of Aline's fingers and toes were tingling, and Beatrice was starting to seem like someone she knew or should have known better, like her college professor girlfriend, who was always looking for new conquests, in both life and career.

"You want to know my secret?" Beatrice asked.

It took Aline a minute to figure out that Beatrice was still talking about the coffee.

"You want to know why it tastes so good?"

"I'm interested," Aline said.

"The secret is time," Beatrice said, picking up the cup she'd poured for herself. "I always take my time, whether it's getting dressed, making coffee, or sewing those wedding gowns."

As she reached into her bag, pulled out a tape recorder, and put it on the edge of the coffee table between them, Aline thought that if Beatrice took as much time with her work as she did getting dressed and making coffee, her brides would be baptizing their children by the time their gowns were done. However, she simply asked, "Do you mind if I record?"

"First," Beatrice began as though she were the one conducting the interview, "remind me again what this is for."

"As I mentioned yesterday," Aline said, "I write for the *Haitian American Weekly*. You made a wedding dress for our editor in chief, Marjorie Voltaire. Do you remember Marjorie?"

Beatrice raised both her hands to her chin, her penciled eyebrows creased in full concentration as though she were trying to channel Marjorie Voltaire into the room.

"Well, Marjorie was so sad to learn you're retiring that she asked me to write this story."

What Marjorie had actually said was, "I hear that the woman who made my wedding dress is giving up the trade. Go talk to her. Maybe we can get a short piece out of it."

"I don't remember that girl," Beatrice said with a sigh of resignation, as though she'd given remembering her best shot and failed, "but I've made a lot of dresses for a lot of girls. In any case, it would have been better for you to write this when I was still working. I could have gotten a few more clients and would have stopped sooner."

Seeing this as an opportunity to officially begin the interview, Aline leaned over and pressed a button on the tape recorder.

"Do you mind if I ask how old you are?"

"Old," Beatrice said.

"Forties?" Aline ventured, even though Beatrice looked much older, late fifties at least.

Beatrice threw her head back and let out an earsplitting laugh, contorting her face in such a way that her skin, had it been cloth, would have taken hours to iron out.

"So you would have liked to retire sooner?" Aline continued.

"Everything happens when it's meant to happen," Beatrice said. "That's what I tell my girls when they think they're either too early or too late in getting married. By the way, are you married?"

"No," Aline said.

"Don't worry," Beatrice said, taking another sip of her coffee. "I'm not going to sit here and tell you what a great institution it is."

"Please tell me why you've chosen to retire now, after all this time," Aline said. "You've been making wedding dresses for many years, is that so?"

"I've been making these dresses since Haiti." Beatrice arched her neck and pushed her head toward Aline's. "In all that time, I've sewn every stitch myself. Never had anyone helping me. Never could stand having anyone in my house for too long. Now it's become too hard. I'm tired."

Beatrice stated this last part flatly, as though it were simply a fact, not a plea for sympathy or pity, which Aline couldn't help but admire.

"Describe for me the process of making a wedding dress," Aline said.

"Well." Beatrice cleared her throat after a series of dry coughs, as sudden and as consistent as a smoker's cough or a lint cough. "My girls—when I say my girls, I mean the girls I make the dresses for—they come here carrying photographs of tall, skinny girls in dresses that cost thousands of dollars. They bring those to me and say, 'Mother'—I make them all call me Mother, it's more respectful that way—they say, 'Mother, this is the dress I must have for my wedding.' It's part of my job to tell them, without making them cry, that they're too short, too wide, or too pregnant for a dress like that, even if I lose money. I don't do this for money. When any of my girls puts on one of my dresses, everyone at that wedding is going to be looking at it. When they're singing 'Here comes the bride,' they're really singing 'Here comes the dress.' And the way I see it, I am that dress. It's like everyone's looking at me."

Now we're getting somewhere, Aline thought. What could she ask next that would get a similarly lengthy response?

"Have you ever been married?"

"You never ask a woman my age a question like that," Beatrice replied.

"The readers might want to know if you've ever made a wedding dress for yourself," Aline said by way of an apology. "Besides, you asked me—"

"It's okay to ask younger women," Beatrice interrupted, "but with a woman like me, you keep that type of question to yourself. I've never wanted to be asked that question. That's why all the girls call me Mother."

Aline wrote on her reporter's pad, "Never married."

Soon, one side of Aline's cassette was near full. As she turned the tape over, Beatrice suddenly suggested that they take a walk down her block so Aline could see it.

"I don't need to do that right now," Aline tried to protest.

But Beatrice was already standing up and walking to her door.

.   .   .

It was a sunny, yet breezy afternoon. There were birds and squirrels skipping on the branches of the tall green ash in front of Beatrice's house. Aside from the child-care center at the end of the block, all the houses looked the same, with red-brick facades, gabled roofs, bow windows on the first floors and sash ones on the top. There were steps leading up from the street to the doorways and a patch of land up front that some fenced in and made into a garden and others cemented into an open driveway.

As she and Aline strolled up and down the block, Beatrice pointed out the residences of her neighbors, identifying them mostly by their owners' professions and nationalities. On the left was the home of the Italian baker and his policewoman wife. Across the street was the house of the elderly Guyanaian dentist and his daughter the bank manager. Further down the block was the Dominican social worker, then the Jamaican schoolteacher, and finally the Haitian prison guard.

Beatrice had another coughing spell in front of the prison guard's house, and when it stopped, her face was somber, her eyes moist.

"Where does he work?" Aline asked, imagining a long commute for Beatrice's sole Haitian neighbor, from some distant correctional facility in upstate New York.

"I knew him in Haiti," Beatrice replied. She raised her fingers toward the Roman shades on the front window, accusingly, it seemed to Aline, but then refused to say anything else. Was he an old friend, Aline wondered, a new enemy, a past love?

"Do the two of you talk?" Aline asked. "Are you friends?"

"Friends?" Beatrice made a loud sucking noise with her tongue and teeth. Before walking away, she waved her hands dismissively at the house, as if wanting to make it disappear.

When they returned to Beatrice's front steps, a few more ash leaves had fallen there. Beatrice reminded herself out loud that she needed to have the higher branches of the green ash trimmed. For she often sat on her stairs in the early evening, she said, completing some details of her work.

Beatrice disappeared into her kitchen as soon as they walked into her house. Aline looked around the living room again, this time for some sign of the mysterious jailer, a photograph, a love or hate letter, some framed memento that she'd missed.

Beatrice returned with the rest of the coffee, still warm from earlier.

"Did you study to do what you're doing now?" she asked Aline, setting down new clean cups.

"Not really," Aline said. "I studied French." Then not sure that Beatrice understood or approved of her college major, she elaborated, "Books, words written by French people over many centuries."

These last few words seemed to clarify nothing, just as they never did for Aline's parents, who ran their church's

day-care center in Somerville, Massachusetts, so Aline
became quiet. She didn't want to tell Beatrice that she'd
simply taken the newspaper internship because it was the
first paid job she was offered after she'd been dumped by
her girlfriend, needing important-sounding work to report
to both her ex—should they ever speak again—and her
folks.

"When you were studying this, what was it, French, did
you learn anything useful?" Beatrice asked offhandedly.

Aline's common sense and her recollection of Marjorie
Voltaire's caveats told her that she was losing control of
the interview. However, it had been such a long time since
anyone had spoken to her with such interest that she
frankly welcomed it.

She was finding it hard now to remember anything
from any of the hundreds of books she'd read in school.
What instantly came to mind, aside from her former professor, was a film of a depth-perception experiment she'd
seen in a Psych 101 class, in which an infant cried when he
was made to crawl over a glass surface with an image of a
deep gorge below. Much had been made of the fact that
the infant had displayed fear of falling into the gorge,
despite not knowing what a gorge was or what it meant to
fall. Aline had thought the experiment cruel and had been
unable to watch most of the class film, though she'd never
been able to forget what little she'd seen.

It was after she babbled the story of the gorge experiment to Beatrice and got no response that she noticed the
sewing kit on Beatrice's lap, a cedar box divided into

several sections, each filled with thimbles, bodkins, pin-cushions, and chatelaines that looked as though they were from another era. Beatrice was searching for something in the box and let out a sigh of relief when she found it. It was a gold thimble with her name carved in microscopic letters on the base and a wreath of tiny wildflowers on the rim.

Beatrice moved the thimble closer to Aline's nose ring, then took turns capping each of her ten fingers with it.

"What are you going to do after you retire?" Aline asked, trying to complete the interview.

"Move, again." Beatrice pressed the thimble between her palms, rolling it up and down as if to warm it.

"Why?" Aline asked.

Beatrice put the thimble back in the box, then set the whole kit down on the ground. She covered her eyes with both hands, then gradually removed her fingers as though to slowly take in the world again.

"We called them choukèt laroze," Beatrice said, the couch's plastic cover squeaking beneath her. "They'd break into your house. Mostly it was at night. But often they'd also come before dawn, as the dew was settling on the leaves, and they'd take you away. He was one of them, the guard."

Beatrice removed her open-toed sandals and raised her feet so Aline could see the soles of her feet. They were thin and sheer like an albino baby's skin.

"He asked me to go dancing with him one night," Bea-trice said, putting her feet back in her sandals. "I had a boyfriend, so I said no. That's why he arrested me. He tied me to some type of rack in the prison and whipped the bottom of my feet until they bled. Then he made me walk home, barefoot. On tar roads. In the hot sun. At high noon. This man, wherever I rent or buy a house in this city, I find him, living on my street."

Beatrice got up and collected the empty coffee cups, piling them on the tray. Aline reached over to help her, but Beatrice gently pushed her hands away.

It was the inevitable question, maybe insulting, but Aline felt she had to ask it. "Are you sure it's the same person?"

Beatrice removed her bronze wig, revealing a line of cotton-white cornrows, curved toward the back of her neck. She raised her hand to her head and scratched her scalp as though to quell a flame there.

"You never look at anyone the way you do someone like this." Beatrice's exasperation was spewing out with the spittle at the side of her mouth. "No one will ever have that much of your attention. No matter how much he'd changed, I would know him anywhere."

"I think she's a bit nutty," Aline said to a gruff and hurried Marjorie Voltaire on her cell phone. She was sitting in her car outside the prison guard's house with her notepad and tape recorder on her lap.

"I'm in a meeting with my photographers, have a pissed-off advertiser on the other line, and the printer's late with this week's edition," Marjorie Voltaire snapped. "Aren't we all a little nutty? I know you're very proud of the fact that you took Psych 101, but I didn't send you there to judge her state of mind. Come back and write what I sent you to write: Bridal Seamstress Retires. Simple."

From the front seat of her car, Aline could see the Roman shades on the barber's front window and the green ash shedding more leaves on Beatrice's porch in one glimpse. The green ash, the only one on the block, was still shaking ever so slightly in the afternoon breeze, letting loose a few more leaves. Beatrice was sitting on the steps in front of her house, watching the street, but mostly watching the leaves drop. It was an odd yet beautiful sight, the leaves seemingly suspended in the air, then falling ever so slowly as if cushioned by air bubbles. It was an image worth closing another type of article with, Aline thought, but in many ways it was so ordinary. It was fall, after all.

Aline was thinking of immediately heading back to the office to type up the story she'd been assigned: BRIDAL SEAMSTRESS RETIRES. SIMPLE. Mercilessly edited by Marjorie Voltaire, it would probably be reduced to a brief anyway, a five-inch announcement. But as she reached over to start her car, she took one final look at the prison guard's house, wondering if there might be something there, a bigger story, one that could earn Marjorie Voltaire's respect. Then something made her pull her hand away from the keys in the ignition. It was the house's mailbox, a small, black, metal box, attached to the brick facade beneath the residence numbers. The mailbox was stuffed, nearly overflowing, as though no one had touched it for a while.

Aline got out of her car and crossed the street, then slowly climbed the steps to the front door. There was a small window, high in the door, but it was covered with what seemed like a piece of construction paper the same linseed color as the door. Flipping through the mailbox's contents with her fingertips, she quickly searched for address labels, a name. She found mostly advertisements: flyers for mechanic shops, neighborhood dry cleaners, restaurants, and supermarket sales; catalogs for women's clothing addressed to "Resident" or "Occupant."

Aline walked down the front steps and stepped back from the house to have another look. The front window was too high for her to peek inside. Besides, it was well covered, with what on closer examination seemed like dark plastic, underneath the Roman shades.

There was a sliding window on the side of the house. It too had a curtain on it, but the window was lower than the others and the curtain was thin and there was a gap between the window frame and the drapery, which would allow her a look inside.

She moved swiftly, but casually, trying as much as possible not to call any attention to herself. If any of the neighbors saw her, she wanted to appear as though she was visiting and not trespassing.

As she raised her body to the window, she took one last look at the street to make sure no one was looking. A group of teenagers strolled by, crowding the sidewalk. They seemed to be on their way home from school, talking and laughing loudly, not paying attention to her.

She waited for them to pass the house, their voices blending with sounds of cars going by; then she stood on the tips of her toes, tilted her head, craned her neck, and looked inside. From where she was standing, she had an angled view of what appeared to be the dining room. The living room, she figured, based on the layout of Beatrice's house, was the room you walked into when you entered the house. There was a wooden staircase leading upstairs, but the dining room itself was empty. The walls were gleaming white, as though they'd just been painted, and the parquet floors looked shiny, but sticky, as if they'd recently been varnished and hadn't dried properly. It didn't appear as though anyone was living there.

The sound of a car pulling into the driveway next door forced Aline to move away from the window. She walked back to the front of the house until she could see Beatrice once more, sitting out on her front steps, sewing.

"Are you looking for someone?" The next-door neighbor was standing in his driveway, leaning against his car and twirling a set of keys, watching Aline. He must be the Jamaican schoolteacher, Aline guessed. The lilt in his voice as he said, "Are you a friend of Dolly's?" confirmed this.

Aline answered, "Dolly?"

"Are you a friend of Dolly's?" he repeated, grinning, as though he would have very much liked her to be.

"Isn't there a man living here?" Aline asked. "A corrections officer?"

"No one's lived here since Dolly Rodriguez," the man said, bouncing his keys from hand to hand. "And that was over a year ago. I know she's trying to sell, but it's hard to do that from Bogotá. She just has to get her butt here and stay a while, if she ever wants to be rid of this place."

"Thank you," Aline said. "I didn't know."

"No sweat," the man replied. He kept waving as she walked away from him. Perhaps he knew she was lying, for only when she made it to Beatrice's front steps did he walk into his own house.

Beatrice had unbraided her cornrows so that her hair, now high and thick, looked like an angry cloud, a swollen halo floating a few inches above her. Aline sat down on the last step, where Beatrice's slippered feet lay, and watched silently as she meticulously stitched the hem of a taffeta wedding slip, possibly her last.

Beatrice said nothing, as if trying not to break her own concentration. When she was done with the hem, her face relaxed and in this late-afternoon light, she seemed as airless as the green ash leaves that had gathered in small heaps around her.

"You're back," she said, gathering the slip on her lap so

that, resting there, it looked like a large animal covered in gauze.

"The house is empty," Aline said.

Beatrice didn't seem shocked, as Aline had expected, or even embarrassed, as Aline had been, facing Dolly Rodriguez's next-door neighbor.

"Of course it's empty," Beatrice said, raising her hands in the air as if to emphasize that it couldn't have been any other way. "That's where he hides out these days, in empty houses. Otherwise he'd be in jail, paying for his crimes."

Beatrice moved the taffeta slip from her lap and gently placed it on the floor, at her side. She was not looking at Aline but was staring at the street, waiting for a few cars to go by before speaking again.

"I think the reason he finds me all the time is because I send notes out to my girls," Beatrice said, keeping her eyes on the street. "I let all my girls know when I move, in case they want to bring other girls to me. That's how he always finds me. It must be. But now I'm not going to send these notes out anymore. I'm not going to make any more dresses. The next time I move, he won't find out where I am."

Growing up poor but sheltered in Somerville, Massachusetts, Aline had never imagined that people like Beatrice existed, men and women whose tremendous agonies filled every blank space in their lives. Maybe there were hundreds, even thousands, of people like this, men and women chasing fragments of themselves long lost to others. Maybe Aline herself was one of them.

These were the people Aline wanted to try to write about now, no matter what Marjorie Voltaire said. And if Marjorie didn't like it, then she would quit and go work somewhere else. She might even return to Somerville and, at last, let her parents learn who she was. Or she might escape to Florida for a while, to avoid eating that five-star-restaurant meal by herself.

But for now, she would simply sit with Beatrice and wait for some time to pass, so that she might see how the green ash leaves looked slowly falling from the tall tree in the very ordinary golden light of dusk.

MONKEY TAILS

(FEBRUARY 7, 1986/FEBRUARY 7, 2004)

Mother and I cowered beneath her cot after a small rock pierced the sheet of plastic she'd draped over our bedroom window the week before as extra protection against the alley mosquitoes. She was winded from all the excitement outside, forcing air out of her lungs while trying to contain a sudden bout of hiccups. Keeping her eyes closed, she felt for the rosary around her neck and between hiccups and deep breaths whispered, "Jesus, Mary, Saint Joseph, please watch over Michel and me."

The sound of a large crowd stomping through the alley between Monsieur Christophe's water station and our house seemed to be what was making the cot rattle, rather than Mother's and my shaking bodies. Above the echoes of drums, horns, bamboo flutes, and conch shells, we heard voices shouting, "Come out, macoutes! Come out, macoutes!" daring members of the Volunteers for National Security militia to appear from wherever they were hiding.

Overnight our country had completely changed. We had fallen asleep under a dictatorship headed by a pudgy thirty-four-year-old man and his glamorous wife. During the night they'd sneaked away—I had to see the television images myself before I could believe it—the wife ornately made up, her long brown hair hidden under a white turban, her carefully manicured fingers holding a long cigarette, the husband at the wheel of the family's BMW, driving his wife and himself to the tarmac of an airport named after his dead father, from whom he'd inherited the country at nineteen, to an American airplane that would carry them to permanent exile in France. The presidential couple's reign had ended, his having lasted fifteen years and hers the span of their six-year marriage. Their departure, however, orphaned a large number of loyal militiamen, who had guarded the couple's command with all types of vicious acts. Now the population was going after those militiamen, those macoutes, with the determination of an army in the middle of its biggest battle to date.

My cousin Vaval, who'd left the house at dawn to catch a camion to the provinces but then had postponed his trip to come back and brief us on what was going on, told us how on his way to the bus depot he had seen a group of people tie one of these militiamen to a lamppost, pour gasoline down his throat, and set him on fire. The flock making its way through the alley behind our house was probably on a similar quest for vengeance, most likely looking for a man called Regulus, who lived nearby. Regulus' eighteen-year-old son, Romain, was my hero and the person whom at that time I considered my best friend.

It didn't take long for the crowd to move past our house. I had to remind myself that these men and women, old and young, meant no harm to people like us, people like Mother, Vaval, and me. Vaval was so certain of this that he was standing out in front of the house watching the crowd, as though it was an ordinary parade going by. Mother, however, whose creed in life was something like "It's harder for trouble to find you under your bed" (yes, I know there are many ways she could have been proven wrong), had thought that it would be best for us to hide. The rock coming through the window reinforced her case. I couldn't help but be frightened. I was twelve years old, and, according to my mother, three months before my birth I had lost my father to something my mother would only vaguely describe as "political," making me part of a generation of mostly fatherless boys, though some of our fathers were still living, even if somewhere else—in the provinces, in another country, or across the alley not acknowledging us. A great many of our fathers had also died in the dictatorship's prisons, and others had abandoned us altogether to serve the regime.

My mother's hiccups subsided. Judging that the crowd had moved a safe enough distance from our house, she raised a corner of her skirt and used it to wipe the sweat from her forehead, crossed herself several times, then crawled out from under the cot. She waited for me to come out, then sat on the cot's edge and dusted a film of white grime from her knees.

"I knew that girl was not sweeping all the way under the beds," my mother said, quickly reverting to her normal griping self, perhaps to erase the image in my mind of her cowering with fear under the cot. The "girl" she was referring to was Rosie, a distant cousin my mother had summoned from the provinces to do such things as cook and wash and sweep under beds, when she'd promised Rosie's poor peasant parents that she'd be sending her to school. In fact, the only education Rosie was getting was from talking to the people who came to buy colas at a busy intersection where my mother stationed her when Rosie wasn't inside the house cooking, washing, and *not* sweeping under the beds. Being madly in love with Rosie—Rosie's bloodline was separate enough from mine that I could have married her had I been older—I didn't blame her at all for the dust balls under the cot, but I knew better than to defend her to my mother, who would have turned her anger at Rosie on me.

All the commotion with the departure of our despised leader and his wife and the crowd passing through the neighborhood had made me hungry. But what I wanted most to do was head over to Romain's house and make sure he was okay. Like us, Romain and his mother had nothing to fear from our angry neighbors. It was Romain's father, Regulus, they wanted. He'd beaten them up and stolen money and property from most of them and had

put many of their relatives in jail or in the grave. In addi-
tion to his other crimes, Regulus had abandoned Romain
when Romain was a month old. Romain had never called
his father Papa but, like everyone else, referred to him as
Regulus, his last name, which Romain didn't even have.

Romain and I had met when I was about eight years old.
His mother and mine had become friends, taking turns visiting each other every evening to catch up at the end of
the day. I would accompany my mother on her visits to his
house, and while our mothers sat inside and chatted, we
would play marbles or kick a soccer ball around out front.

Unlike many of the older boys, Romain didn't have
many friends and didn't seem to resent having to play with
a runt like me. In fact, he even appeared to like it and came
around to my house most Sunday afternoons to ask my
mother if he could take me to a kung fu movie or for a bike
ride on Champs de Mars plaza.

Our mothers had a falling-out one day—neither Romain
nor I was ever able to find out from either of them what it
was about—and I stopped visiting Romain's house with my
mother and he stopped coming around to ask my mother's
permission to take me places. Our outings became less fre-
quent, but every once in a while we'd plot to meet somewhere and then proceed to a karate flick, especially if it was
a new Bruce Lee.

Romain knew what it was like to be an only child. And
maybe this is why he always watched out for me, stepped

in if I was in a scuffle with some other kid from the neighborhood, slipped me some of his mother's money now and then for candy and ice cream, and invited me over to his house whenever his mother was away. His maid, Auberte, would prepare whatever I wanted to eat, whether it was good for me or not. While we ate Auberte's delicious fried sweets, I would listen to Romain talk and talk, mostly quoting lines from books I'd never read and writers I'd never heard of. Even though I rarely understood everything he said, I was grateful that he was speaking to me, like a peer, like a man.

Looking back now, I realize how much I needed someone like Romain in my life. He must have felt this too. Come to think of it, aside from Rosie and Vaval, who were always too busy with my mother's chores to spend much time with me, Romain was my only friend.

When Mother and I finally made our way outside, we found Vaval and Rosie out front, commenting to each other on the procession of marchers that had just gone by. Before she realized that my mother and I were watching her, Rosie bent down and picked up a few sprigs of greenery and flowers that the crowd had strewn along its path. She held them up to her nose and inhaled what was left of their fragrance, even though they were dusty and soiled and had been trampled flat before she'd gotten to them.

Vaval too walked out to the street and collected a few cast-off beer and rum bottles. Putting an end to their contemplation, my mother ordered them both to go back into the house and find something more useful to do. Rosie somehow managed to interrupt Mother long enough to point out that across the alley Monsieur Christophe's tap station had been dismantled by the passing crowd and his faucets were pumping free water faster than a newly slaughtered pig pumps blood. A different crowd was emerging now, a crowd of maids, menservants, and indentured children, restavèks, carrying all sorts of vessels, including buckets, water jugs, earthen jars, calabashes, and even chamber pots, to gather the precious water. Mother ordered Rosie and Vaval to hurry up and collect as much water as they could for our house.

At my mother's side, I tried to calculate how much money Monsieur Christophe was losing as each of his six faucets and their missing handles pumped out several gallons of water per minute. Usually, he would sell a bucket of water for twenty centimes, to everyone except my mother, who could get it from him for less. When cassavas and colas, breads or mangoes or straw hats didn't sell, my mother would buy a bucket of water from Monsieur Christophe and have Rosie walk through the streets downtown, reselling the water by the cup to thirsty people. Now Monsieur Christophe, a scowling, cinnamon-colored man who was only slightly taller than I, was trying to shut off the main valve that would keep any more water from gushing forth. But someone had walked away with the large knob that controlled the water flow, leaving Monsieur Christophe and a group of other men who worked for him with no choice but to try to slide the large knobless tube shut by force.

"Michel, come over here." Monsieur Christophe spotted me during one of those times when he turned away from the valve in despair. "We need more hands."

It was a new day, I thought. The number of people marching through the alleys when it wasn't carnival or Rara season without being shot down by the macoutes had confirmed it. What right did our resident water hoarder have to order me to do anything? Still, I walked over. The big shove from my mother also helped me make up my mind. Besides, there was always the possibility that things could return to the way they'd been the night before—the television could have an image of the presidential couple coming back—and the crowds could ungather. Also, there were people with shops in our neighborhood, people like Monsieur Christophe, who had always been and would always be powerful, maintaining authority through control of water or bread or some other important resource, as Romain might say, no matter what was going on politically.

I hated joining Monsieur Christophe's valve-shutting operation because it would delay my trip to Romain's. In any case, I didn't feel I was helping very much, with so many stronger boys and men already offering ideas, pulling out makeshift tools they always carried in their pockets, enjoying the entire affair much more than I was. I wanted to let the water flow. There was probably so much blood being shed in different parts of the country that morning, the blood of militiamen at the hands of former

victims, the blood of former victims at the hand of militiamen battling for their lives. Maybe the water could be a
cleansing offering to the gods on behalf of all the dead, no
matter what their political leanings had been.

But I wasn't thinking like this back then. I simply
wanted to go off and visit my friend. I only think all this
now, as a thirty-year-old man, lying in bed next to my
pregnant wife, watching as the clock moves toward midnight, toward her due date.

I reluctantly joined the group of men squatting around
stupid Monsieur Christophe's valve, trying to shut it off,
but I spent most of my time watching more and more people arrive to collect the free water, more and more street
children slipping beneath the taps for impromptu showers
and being shoved aside so the water might be used for
more important purposes. My mother was standing across
the alley observing me, and each time our eyes met, she
would give me a scolding glance for not participating
more. Still, I could tell she was proud of me. For once I was
surrounded by men, doing men's work. She seemed happy
that Monsieur Christophe had thought to include me and
even happier still that he would occasionally single me out
for some task, like holding a rag or a screwdriver, a task I
would share with Tobin, Monsieur Christophe's openly
acknowledged son.

"Strange how blessings come," I imagined my mother
saying. Strange too how people with means can make the

less fortunate feel special by putting them to work. As much as I loved my mother, I would have easily traded that satisfied grin on her face for a word, any word, even an insult, from Romain.

My opportunity for escape came when my mother joined Rosie and Vaval in collecting just a little more water for the house. She had strolled across the alley, carrying two small jugs, and had gone back inside the house to put them away once they were full. I handed Monsieur Christophe's son Tobin, a pale-skinned fellow twelve-year-old, the screwdriver I was holding. And at a moment when Monsieur Christophe was concentrating on some complicated procedure that required him to be as close to the valve as possible, I ran.

There was a different feel to our neighborhood for sure. People were walking around looking dazed, exchanging bits of information they were gathering from the radio and television and from one another. Like Rosie, many were collecting shrubs from the ground and waving them in the air. Some of the men were wearing red bandannas around their heads and swinging sticks and tree branches while pouring rum and beer on one another. Others were dancing and performing somersaults but stopping occasionally to yell slogans or phrases they had held too long in their chests: "We are free" or "We will never be prisoners again."

The bells of the nearby cathedral were chiming non-stop even as several people were shouting, through windows and above the loud horns of passing cars, that the tomb of the pudgy dictator's father, from whom the son had inherited the country, had just been excavated by demonstrators. An early rumor had it that the son had carried the father's bones with him into exile, but the people who'd opened the father's crypt believed they had the bones and were parading them downtown, skull and all.

Graffiti were going up everywhere. Down with the departed president and his wife! Down with poverty! Down with suffering! Down with everything you can imagine.

From the radio reports that were being broadcast at the loudest possible volume from every house, I gathered that the homes of former government officials and the abandoned mansions of the president and his wife were being ransacked, with protesters carrying away everything from tiles to toilet bowls to toothbrushes. There was the stench of kerosene and burning tires wafting through the air. It was only a matter of time before the rubber smell would be replaced with that of flesh.

The doors were bolted tight at Romain's mother's house. Only when I got there did I remember that Romain's mother was away on one of her business trips, buying cloth and women's undergarments in Curaçao for resale. Like my mother, Romain's was a business-minded woman, even though she was operating on a larger scale than my mother was.

Romain's aunt Vesta came to the door and opened it a crack to check out my face. I was in love with Vesta too, enraptured by her long neck and legs, which she displayed freely in thigh-stroking skirts. Vesta hastily let me in. She wanted me to give her a detailed account of what was going on out in the streets, and I did. But in the end all she really wanted to know was whether or not Regulus had been caught.

"I don't think so," I said.

"The old man's probably far away from here now." Romain's voice boomed inside the room where Vesta had her bed, a table, and a radio from which a taped message from the exiled president was being disseminated.

"I have decided to transfer the destiny of the nation into the hands of the military," the dictator fils declared in a droning nasal voice that sounded almost the same as his father's, whose daylong speeches were constantly rebroadcast on the radio each year on the anniversary of his death. It was then reported that six rich men, most of them military officers, would take control of the country.

"It will be more of the same," Vesta said. "Nothing will change."

Romain, who'd been standing there as still as a rock through the entire announcement, motioned for me to walk through the white lace curtain that separated Vesta's room from the rest of the house. Romain was slight but limber, like the kung fu masters. It was clear that he hadn't bathed, combed his hair, or changed his clothes since the last time I'd seen him, three days before. He was unshaven, barefoot, and scratching his thin legs through his imported jeans. His sunken, bloodshot eyes seemed as though they were struggling to blink, showing that he hadn't slept much either.

Romain's mother's beautiful two-story house was her unconditional gift to him, compensation—his word—for his having to take her last name. As we entered the blush-rose living room and settled down on the sofa, Auberte trailed us and asked if we wanted some refreshments.

Romain replied, "Pi ta," later, and waved Auberte away, but she paid no attention to him and brought us each a glass of freshly squeezed lemonade and a large piece of buttered bread served on a colorful tray covered with images of Curaçao's beaches, beaches with names like Barbara, Marie, and Jeremi.

And yes, I was in love with Auberte too. Sometimes I had dreams of Rosie, Vesta, and Auberte coming into the room I shared with my mother and sending my mother away only to fight one another for the honor of devirginizing me.

My wife stirs in our bed now, trying not to move from the one position she's able to sleep in these days, on her back. My son, you are also lying on your side, I imagine, resting for your imminent journey to us. (You will have to tell me one day what it is you were really doing.)

Listen to your mother now as she says to me, "Michel, are you still talking into that cassette? Go to sleep. If the baby comes tomorrow I'll need you rested."

And listen as I, your father, reply, "Just another minute."

And listen now as your mother says, half jokingly, I hope, "I wish I was one of those women you *only* dreamed of sleeping with," then goes back to sleep.

Now we return to Romain.

Romain did not drink the overly sweetened lemonade Auberte brought him. He was jittery, his fingers shaking as he bit into his bread. He put the rest of the bread down, got up and paced around the room, and pressed his face against the wall, coming short of banging his forehead against it. Then he walked over to the large television set on the coffee table, reached over as if to turn it on, then held himself back. Instead he sat down, picked up his lemonade once more, and stared into the glass at the thick layer of brown sugar refusing to melt at the bottom.

"When will your mother be back?" I asked him.

"Couple of days," he said, raising his eyes from the glass. Then he paraphrased Voltaire the way he always did whenever he was served anything with too much sugar in it.

"C'est à ce prix qu'ils mangent du sucre en Europe," he recited. That's the price of their eating sugar in Europe.

While studying for his BAC exams, Romain had become too distracted by the French literature segments, going off to read entire books excerpted in his lessons. He would fall behind in class, while seeking other sources on the same themes until he'd mastered them. In the end, he gave up school entirely to study on his own. By way of explanation for ending his studies, he had simply cited someone else to his mother—I would later learn that it was Socrates—"Know thyself and you will know the world of the gods."

But just then, when he looked at the sweet juice, which I was enjoying very much myself, saying "C'est à ce prix qu'ils mangent du sucre en Europe," I replied, "Okay, your majesty," feeling glad that at least his father wasn't the only thing on his mind.

"I'm sharing with you Voltaire's words," he said. "I tell you that in Europe they eat sugar with our blood in it and you mock me with a colonial title."

I realized then that it was going to be business as usual, just an ordinary Romain conversation, and so I said, "It seems to me we consume a lot of sugar here too. Does that mean we're drinking our own blood?"

He laughed and said, "Imbecile, you're like that baby pig who deigns to ask its mother how come her nose is so big and ugly. Let me be the mother and tell you, 'Pig, son, one day you'll find this out for yourself.'"

We both laughed. Then his face grew somber and he said, "You know, I'm not listening to the radio or watching television that much. Tante Vesta is, but I'm not."

"Why watch television or listen to the radio?" I said. "If you want to know what's happening, hit the béton, the pavement, go out into the streets."

I was feeling cocky, brazen. I'd ventured out when Romain had not. I'd slipped away from my mother's grasp to do something she disapproved of, visit with Romain. I felt I had an edge on him. I could now tell him about things he hadn't yet witnessed, things that were going on out there in our new world.

"I know I shouldn't be feeling this," he said, brushing aside my attempted boast by simply ignoring it, "but I can't help it. I'm a little worried about Regulus. I know the old man isn't going to sit around waiting for them to get him, but it seems that people like him are going to die very painful deaths."

"When was the last time you saw Regulus?" I asked.

"Last May eighteenth," he said. "He was marching in the Flag Day parade on the national palace grounds with all those other macoutes. I went to watch the stupid parade, just to spot him."

"They probably won't find him," was all I could think to say. "He has so many women. One of them will hide him good. Maybe he'll cross the border, go to the Dominican Republic."

"Maybe," Romain said, halfheartedly agreeing to all those possibilities. Maybe Regulus would survive and emerge from all this a new man, repent for all his sins, reclaim all his children, offer them his name—if they still wanted it—beg their forgiveness, both for what he'd done to them and for what he had done to his country.

My mother popped into my head once again. By now she'd probably noticed that I was gone and was furiously looking for me, ordering Rosie and Vaval to join the search. She would think I was out running around with the demonstrators, trying to discover where they would go next, see who they'd find and what they'd do.

"What's the matter?" Romain asked.

"I'm worried about my mother," I confessed. "She might be fretting about me."

"Twelve years old," he said, "and still Mama's baby. I'm going to make you a man today. We're going to do like those guys, like Regulus. We're going to escape."

We didn't tell Vesta where we were going. We simply hurried past her, Romain mumbling that we'd be right back.

"Come back here!" Vesta yelled as we rushed out of the house. "Do you know what's going on out there? Come back!"

As we sprinted away, I asked Romain, "Where are we going?"

"If we had someplace in mind," he said, "then we'd be going on a trip, not escaping."

Most of the shops near Romain's house were closed even as the streets were growing more and more crowded. On the way to the bus depot, we found ourselves in the middle of a mock funeral procession with a group of "pallbearers" carrying two wooden coffins, one for the president and the other for his wife. Some of the men in the crowd donned priest's cassocks while young women in black dresses pretended to be sobbing and fainting from inconsolable grief. Among the mock mourners were a few waving blue denim uniforms, which they claimed to have stripped off fleeing macoutes.

We made our way out of the crowd and down an alley into a quieter street, where we found a taxi. Romain jumped in and told the driver, "We'd like to go to La Sensation Hotel."

"That's not going to be easy," the driver said, "with all the people on the streets."

"Take all the shortcuts you know," Romain said. "You'll be paid well."

The drive to La Sensation confirmed that we couldn't escape what was going on, short of leaving the city or the country. Everywhere we went, even through the narrowest side streets, byways, back ways, there were people jumping out of corners, waving flags, ripping old posters of the president and his wife, and carrying containers of kerosene, hoping to find a macoute to punish.

When we finally made it to the walled oasis of the hotel, Romain sent me ahead to wait for him in the garden while he settled things with the driver; then we walked over to the front desk together, only to find out that all the rooms were booked, mostly by desperate foreign journalists who were due to arrive within the next twenty-four hours. Romain had been counting on a former classmate who worked as a porter at the hotel to get him a room, where we would hide out until things calmed down. Our escape was going to be financed by Romain's mother, who left him a big wad of cash whenever she went away.

Surprising even myself, I suddenly wanted to go home. I was missing my mother. What if she got so worried that she lost her mind, went running down every street in the capital screaming my name? What if she thought I was dead and my body taken to a mass grave?

Romain's friend was nowhere to be found, and the pretty young woman at the check-in counter gave us such a disdainful look that it seemed she wouldn't have offered us a room even if one had been available.

There was nothing preventing us from sitting here a while and having a drink, though, was there? Romain said. After that we'd go home.

We walked through the lobby, down a flight of stairs to a table under a large umbrella by the side of the heart-shaped pool. A man wearing a dark suit and a bow tie asked us what we wanted to drink. Romain ordered a Coke and so did I. It seemed like such a stupid thing to come all this way for, a Coke.

Romain looked up toward the steep hills above the hotel, and higher still at the row of mountains in the distance. A cloud was passing over the nearest and most prominent one, Mòn Lopital. Then, just as suddenly, the cloud moved on and the sky was as blue as cornflowers again.

Watching me staring up at the mountains, Romain said, "Imagine, a mountain named Hospital. Maybe we should go there."

We had already failed at our small adventure. We were certainly doomed to botch a larger escapade, like a complete retreat to Mòn Lopital. Still, I replied, "Okay," hoping that Romain wouldn't want to follow through with that particular idea.

While we were sipping our Cokes, watching the fizzy dark liquid rise through the straws, a man about Romain's age hesitantly wandered over to our table and sat down. Romain seemed relieved to see him. The man was meticulous-looking, clean-shaven, and tense. He shook Romain's hand, nodded in my direction, then made some guarded remarks about the new political situation, how the hotel was going to lose a lot of its faithful clientele, the call girls, and the macoutes who'd hired them.

Romain casually said, "It must be rough, camarade."

Then the man looked over at me, then back at Romain as though there was something he wanted to tell Romain but wasn't sure I should also hear it.

Finally Romain said, "Man, it's okay." Then I realized there was a larger purpose to our coming to that particular hotel. As with everything else with Romain, this too was not simple.

"You can tell me in front of the little guy," Romain said, lowering his head to sip more of his Coke. "Is he here?"

"No, man. I'm sorry," the man said. And he looked truly regretful, even sympathetic. "He didn't come here. Maybe he went somewhere else."

The man's eyes wandered toward the heart-shaped pool and he shifted uncomfortably in his seat. "It's pretty busy. Sorry you couldn't get a room. We've got to take advantage while we can."

With that, he got up and walked away. Romain kept his head down, kept on sipping his Coke. I should have been too young to understand what was going on, but I did. Twelve years for a boy like me, a boy without a father, a boy with a mother who tried to protect me so much that her actions incited me to go out and discover everything myself, was like twenty years for another kind of boy.

"He sometimes brought women here," Romain said. "I used to follow him here. I thought he might have come here today."

"Who, your father?" I asked.

I don't know why, but every now and then I would ask a dumb question like that, demand an explanation for something I already knew.

"No," Romain snapped, "*your* father, Christophe."

I don't think he even realized why he said it. He was impatient, angry. His nerves were raw. Besides, it wasn't as if I hadn't suspected it. Unaware that I was paying attention, people had often whispered things around me, from the girls in the neighborhood who coyly commented how much I looked like Tobin, the child of the wife, the "inside" child, to even Tobin himself, who was sometimes kind to me and sometimes refused to look me in the eye as though we were rivals, to the wife who refused to ever come anywhere near the tap station in order to avoid facing her husband's indiscretions and their living results. Still, it was too painful for me to be reminded that I had a father who lived and worked so close to me and still didn't call me his son. I didn't understand why my mother had to struggle so much to earn money when she could have asked him for it, why she had to force Rosie into virtual slavery to keep us afloat. I didn't understand why Christophe hadn't offered my mother money to feed and clothe me, why he only sold her water at a discount and did not offer it to her outright since it was water that I, his son, could also use.

As I sat there with Romain with the straw separated from the Coke bottle yet still hanging out of his mouth, it wasn't the shock of hearing Christophe declared my father yet again that made me cry. I was simply ashamed to be considered a dishonorable secret.

Romain tried to reach over and stroke my head, but I shoved his hand away. I wanted to grab one of the Coke bottles and smash it against his skull, but I knew he would catch the bottle before it could hurt him.

He had brought me here, he'd said, to make me a man. Was this what he meant? Did he think that seeing his own murderous father hiding out in a low-grade hotel to keep from being burned alive would illustrate what kind of man I ought not to be? Was telling me, reminding me, about Christophe in this blunt, off-the-cuff manner his way of teaching me that I shouldn't want to be too much like Christophe either? Or was it simply Romain's way of forcing me to accept what he was about to do?

It was becoming clear to me that Romain was leaving, going off someplace where I couldn't follow him.

"The taxi's waiting for you outside," he told me. "He'll get you back to your mother."

I was too angry at him then to ask him where he was going. I didn't care.

"I'm leaving the country," he said. "I'm getting out tonight."

"But you didn't do anything." I heard myself sobbing, but I didn't know whether I was crying for Romain and Regulus or for Christophe and myself.

"I just can't stay here," Romain said.

"What about your mother?" I asked. "What about Regulus?"

"I'll get in touch with my mother when I reach where I'm going," he said. "As for Regulus, he's not my problem."

And then it was very obvious to me, starting with the way his hands were shaking and his frowns were sinking deeper into his sweating forehead, that Regulus had always been his problem, the biggest problem of his life.

"Go on now," he said. "The taxi's waiting for you."

I slowly got up and walked away, counting each step up the staircase leading to the lobby and then down the driveway where the taxi was waiting. I never looked back.

In the taxi, I lay down on the backseat and closed my eyes, shutting out everything, all the noise, the chants, the crowds out on the street. The car moved slowly and the roads were bumpy, but I didn't care.

Given all that was happening—the looting of homes and businesses of former government allies, the lynching, burning, and stoning of the macoutes, the thousands of bodies that were suddenly being discovered in secret rooms at the city morgues and in mass graves on the outskirts of the capital—it would have been heartless of my mother to punish me, and she didn't. Instead she yelled at Rosie and Vaval for not watching me closely enough, for letting me wander away.

"Soon after you went off," my mother said with a severe yet knowing look, an almost kind look, "Monsieur Christophe managed to get his water turned off, but not before everyone in the neighborhood got enough to use for days in case the situation takes a bad turn and we're all trapped inside our houses, like in the old days before you were born, under the father."

"The father?" I asked dumbly.

I knew she meant the dictator father of the dictator son, but somehow I wanted to offer her an opening into a conversation that even then I knew we'd never have.

Though it was still light outside, I went to bed, trying to give the impression that it was the country's political problems that were disturbing me. I'd let my mother keep her secret; I didn't want her to feel like a liar.

That night we fell asleep to the sound of gunfire, sometimes from around the corner and sometimes in the distance. My mother and I slept on opposite sides of her room, on the floor.

When we woke up the next morning, Vaval had more news to report, this time with Rosie chiming in. A group of young men had spotted Regulus sneaking back into his house in the middle of the night to collect some of his belongings. They had cornered him, and to avoid being taken by them, Regulus had shot himself in the head.

I remained curled on the floor and I listened, hoping that Romain was too far away to ever hear of this. Lying there, I remembered something Romain had told me three days before. Rumors had been circulating that the president and his wife might be fleeing the country. The president had gone on television to deny the rumors, saying he was as "unyielding as a monkey's tail."

I didn't know much about monkeys back then, except for a proverb that said if you teach a monkey how to throw stones, it will throw the first one at your head. So I asked Romain to tell me about monkeys' tails.

Monkeys with short tails live on the ground, he'd said, and those with longer tails make their homes closer to the sky, in high trees. Some tree monkeys have tails that are longer than their bodies, tails that they use to swing from tree to tree. We'd both laughed, wondering which kind of monkey's tail our president had imagined himself to be.

"He was a short-tailed one, but now he's a long-tailed one," Romain had said. "He's looking for another tree."

It had seemed impossible then that after fifteen years, a man who'd inherited a lifelong presidency at age nineteen would ever abandon it. But it also hadn't seemed possible that Romain too could disappear and never be heard from again.

. . .

My mother is dead now. One day she collapsed from what was said to be a heart attack, but what I believe was her heart shattering into little pieces because, unlike me, she had loved Christophe and suffered quietly from his not loving her back. I have no proof of this, of course, for my mother was a stern and guarded woman who never would have taken a young boy, even as he became a man, as a confidant. Soon after my mother died, I left Haiti, at twenty, turning over my mother's house to Rosie and Vaval.

I don't know what's become of Romain. I haven't seen or heard from him since that day at the hotel. His aunt Vesta moved out of the neighborhood soon after Regulus died, and his mother never returned from her business trip. I don't even know whether Romain's still alive or dead.

Monsieur Christophe remains very much alive, Rosie and Vaval tell me when I call now and then to check on them, but he has retired and has turned the tap station and other businesses he's since acquired over to his son Tobin.

To everyone who asks me about my father, I tell and retell the myth that my mother so carefully crafted and guarded for me, that my father perished before I was born, lost his life to something "political."

As for you, my son, your myth is this: it's now past midnight; if you're born today, on this, the anniversary of the day that everything changed for me, on the day that I became a man, your name will be Romain, after my first true friend.

THE FUNERAL SINGER

WEEK 1

Rézia, the owner of Ambiance Créole, the sole Haitian restaurant on the Upper West Side of Manhattan, recites a long speech from the class manual:

"Four scones and seven tears ago, our fathers blew up this condiment . . ."

Odd, but Rézia doesn't have a lisp when she attempts to speak English. Everything just gets mixed up in her mouth, like a birdcall in a storm.

Rézia always carries a white muslin handkerchief. As it flaps back and forth, ever so abruptly, it releases more and more of its vetiver fragrance, all the while looking like a kite that she's using to send messages far away.

In spite of Rézia's vetiver, the air in the classroom is scorching and it stings. The air conditioner has stopped humming as if to listen to us talk.

Mariselle, who's shaped like a pencil even in her heavy French suit, stands up in a perfectly straight line and, in her deep voice that sounds like two people, simply states her name. She says it so quickly that it sounds shorter, as though she's given herself a nickname, solely for the purposes of the class.

She's asked to repeat her name. After a third time, she announces each syllable and they merge into two beautiful words, Mari Sèl, Salt Mary or Solitary Mary. You're tempted to add "Pray for us" and I do, under my breath. I can't stop watching the way she tugs at her thick, curly hair each time she opens her mouth, and I can see her scalp rise and fall as she pulls and releases, pulls and releases.

I wish I could sing to introduce myself. Perhaps everyone would be listening too hard to look at me.

I would sing "Brother Timonie." It's a song my father, a fisherman, used to sing whenever he thought a storm was coming.

I'd begin by asking everyone to pretend they were rowing with me, and I'd sing, *Brother Timonie, row well, my friend. Don't you see we're in trouble? Brother Timonie, the wind's blowing hard. And we must make it back to land.*

This is not the first time I've called on Brother Timonie. At least it's not the first time I've tried.

I asked my father once, Who was Brother Timonie?

He didn't know. Maybe a fisherman who died at sea. Most of the songs he knew were about people who'd died at sea.

When I stand to speak, tapping my feet against my chair, the teacher decides to turn my introduction into an inquisition.

"And what do you do?" Her voice hisses, but is flat, never rising or falling.

I do nothing, I want to say. Not yet. I have been expelled from my country. That's why I'm in this class at twenty-two years old.

Once we're all done, the teacher presents herself, saying, "I'm June. You can call me June. If you pay attention and study hard, the test will be a piece of cake and you'll all be considered high school graduates in no time." She looks young and beefy and flat-chested and sits on the desk with her bare cream legs dangling in front of us. She doesn't know what an enormous vow she's made. A diploma in no time? It's like those lawyers who promise green cards in a few weeks.

Rézia nicknames her "Flat Tit" when she notices how like little dandelion buds her breasts look in her pleated strapless sundress. Mariselle is Mother Mary and I'm "the baby funeral singer." I am one of the few professional funeral singers of my generation. At least I was.

WEEK 2

When I was a girl in Léogâne, some days my mother and I would play telephone. We'd tie two empty condensed-milk cans to the ends of a long rope and sing to each other from far away. Sometimes I'd hide inside the house, under our cedar table, and she'd remain outside, but we could still hear each other, without shouting.

During carnival, we'd use our telephone rope for a may-pole dance. We'd skip around each other and duck under the ropes, taking turns at being the maypole and the dancer. We always thought, or she always thought, we were weaving the wind, plaiting it into a braid as thick as the rainbows that were sometimes above our heads.

Whenever she got tired of playing, my mother would look up at the clouds and say, "Look, Freda, Papa's listening to us up there. He's eating coconut with God and he's making a cloud for us with coconut meat."

I thought her mind was gone whenever she said things like that. She also embroidered clouds on pieces of cloth, tiny crimson cirrus threads.

My father used to look at the way the sunset outshone the clouds to decide what the sea would be like the next day. A ruby twilight would mean a calm sea, but a blood-red dawn might spoil everything.

WEEK 3

Blue is the only color I was able to see whenever I was at sea with my father. For a while we forgot there were other colors. Oh, I remembered yellow too, yellow like the sun almost going down.

"Yellow as in sunflowers and marigolds," Rézia observes, fanning herself with her handkerchief and smothering us with vetiver.

"Marigolds, the flower of a thousand lives," Mariselle adds. She puffs on her long, thin Gauloises, covering the filtered tips with her mandarin-red lipstick.

"Yellow like my boyfriend," Rézia says, "the man of a thousand lies."

The teacher shows us a picture of a painting full of sunflowers and says, "Look how there are no dead spots in this painting."

Life is full of dead spots.

I used to wear only new black dresses so I could blend in at the funerals where I sang. Now I wear used clothes, "Kennedys," in rainbow colors, and a red headband around my head, to brighten my dead spots.

WEEK 4

It was Rézia's idea that she, Mariselle, and I go to her restaurant after class. We didn't always understand what was going on in the classroom and, being the only Haitians, we thought we might be able to explain certain lessons to one another, like the grammatical rules for present perfect, which at first I thought meant perfect presents or matchless gifts.

Flowered plastic sheaths were draped over the tables in the dining room, but Rézia would uncover one table so we could drink on the new-looking wooden surface. The walls around us were covered with bright little paintings, portraits of young boys playing with tops and marbles and flying kites, old men casting nets in the ocean, women walking barefoot to the market with large baskets on their heads. There was a dusty fan overhead that Rézia said was only turned on when the cook burned the food and she needed to air out the place. We put on the fan and sat with our knees touching because the table was so small. Only Mariselle would pull her chair away, putting a few inches between us and herself.

I was the one who started it one night over a bottle of urine-colored rum from Rézia's pantry. Mariselle would have only red wine, small bottles of Pinot Noir, which she brought herself.

"I used to play telephone with my mother. . . . I forgot all colors except blue when I went fishing with my father. . . . I was asked to sing at the national palace. . . ."

I thought exposing a few details of my life would inspire them to do the same and slowly we'd parcel out our sorrows, each walking out with fewer than we'd carried in.

WEEK 5

Before my father was arrested, the president of the republic would drive through my town on New Year's Eve and throw money from the window of his big shiny black car. Sun rays would wrap themselves around the brand-new coins, making them glow like glass. When we heard that the president was coming, we would clean our entire house, dust our cedar table, and my father would stay home from the sea in case the president chose to get out of the car and walk into our house, to offer us something extra, a bag of rice, a pound of beans, a gallon of corn oil, a promise of future entrance to the medical school or the agricultural school in Damien, something that would have bought our loyalty forever, so that twenty, thirty, forty years after he was long dead, we might still be saying, "Things were hard, but we once had a president who gave me a sack of rice, some beans, and a gallon of cooking oil. It was the first and last time anyone in power gave me anything." As if this sack of rice, this pound of beans, this gallon of cooking oil were the gold, silver, and bronze medals in the poverty Olympics.

WEEK 6

Two trees, 10 feet apart.

The teacher writes this on the board, turning around to look at our baffled faces. We've all grown accustomed to the suffocating heat in the classroom. All of us except her. She wears as few pieces of clothing as possible, yet still sweats so much that she must cover her hands in chalk dust to reduce her prints on the board.

Two trees, 10 feet apart. Taller tree, 50 feet tall, casts a 20-foot shadow. Shorter tree casts a 15-foot shadow. The sun's shining on each tree from the same angle. How tall is the shorter tree?

It sounds like a riddle that could take a lifetime to solve. We have too much on our minds to unravel these types of mysteries. M'bwè pwa.

"We're not God," Rézia says, lowering her head onto the restaurant table. The bottoms of our glasses have begun to stain the exposed wood, circles touching and overlapping. "Who are we to know how tall a tree should be?"

WEEK 7

Tonight we cook an entire meal together. Mariselle fries the plantains and ends up with a hot-oil burn on the knuckle of her middle finger. Rézia makes the meat, stewed goat. I cook the rice with pigeon peas.

We talk about what brought us here.

Mariselle left because her husband, a painter, had painted an unflattering portrait of the president, which was displayed in a gallery show. He was shot leaving the show.

I was asked to leave the country by my mother because I wouldn't accept an invitation to sing at the national palace. But I also left because long ago my father had disappeared. He'd had a fish stall at the market. One day, one macoute came to take it over and another one took my father away. When my father returned, he didn't have a tooth left in his mouth. In one night, they'd turned him into an old, ugly man. The next night he took his boat out to sea and, with a mouth full of blood, vanished forever.

I remember the exact moment I learned about my father's disappearance. I was lying in bed when I felt the thin cotton sheet covering my body rise. My mother hadn't brought any light into the room, but I could see her clearly, a splinter of moonlight reflected in the tears falling down her face.

"Your papa's across the waters, lòt bò dlo," she had whispered. And in my head had sprouted images of my father lost at sea, rowing farther and farther away until he became as small as a leaf bobbing on the crest of the most distant wave. This is when I began to sing. So he could hear me singing his songs from the crest of that wave.

This is Rézia's story: When she was a girl, her parents couldn't afford to keep her, so they sent her to live with an aunt who ran a brothel. They lived in three rooms behind the brothel and that's where Rézia spent most of her time. One night when she was sleeping, a uniformed man walked in. She dug herself into the bed, but it did no good, so she passed out.

"I can always make myself faint when I'm afraid," Rézia says, fanning the smoke from the pots away from her face. "When I woke up in the morning, my panties were gone. My aunt and I never spoke about it. But on her deathbed she asked for my forgiveness. She said this man had threatened to put her in prison if she didn't let him have me that night."

WEEK 8

Mariselle brings in newspapers that we scour for news from home. She reads one report about a group of armed exiles, a New York–based militia, planning an invasion.

Another about a radio reporter in Port-au-Prince being arrested and taken to the Casernes Dessalines barracks for "questioning." Mariselle reads all this to us in a deep, well-paced voice that sounds like it should be on the radio. When she comes across a name she recognizes, she puts the paper down, closes her eyes, and wipes her lipstick off with the back of her hand.

"I went to school with his brother," she says. "His father and mine were friends."

WEEK 9

We fail our practice tests, except Rézia, who gets seventy percent, enough to pass.

"It's not normal," I complain. "We studied as much as you."

"Listen to the baby funeral singer," Mariselle says, wrapping her manicured hands around the neck of her dark green wine bottle. "You have so much time ahead to redo these things, retake these tests, reshape your whole life."

WEEK 10

We drink too much and stay too long at the restaurant. Mariselle and I have grown used to the idea that we may never get diplomas out of the class.

Mariselle uncorks her second Pinot Noir of the evening. Rézia and I stick to the rum. We like the fiery, bitter taste and the way it makes us foggy right away. I know I'm ruining my voice, but who cares?

The people inside the little paintings are beginning to sway back and forth for the first time. Or is it my head that's dancing? They walk past the borders and merge with our shadows on the wall.

"Let's talk about something cheerful," Rézia says. Her voice is slurred and she sounds sleepy. She's the most drunk of the three of us, consuming more spirits in celebration for passing yet another practice test that Mariselle and I have failed.

"How does a person become a funeral singer, anyway?" Mariselle asks. She throws her hands across my shoulders. Cigarette ashes rain on my orange Salvation Army dress.

The first time I ever sang in public was at my father's memorial Mass. I sang "Brother Timonie," a song whose cadence rises and falls, like the waves of the ocean. I sang it through my tears, and later people would tell me that my sobs reminded them of the incoming tide. From that moment on I became a funeral singer.

Every time there was a funeral in Léogâne, I was asked to sing. I would sing my father's fishing songs and sometimes improvise my own, right there, next to the coffin, in front of the family, at the funeral home or at the church. At other times, I would sing "Ave Maria" or "Amazing Grace," if the family requested them. But I was always appreciated and well compensated.

"Tell me something cheerful," Rézia objects with a mouth full of rice. "Enough about funerals. Enough!"

"Jackie Kennedy came to Haiti last year." Mariselle perks up. She drops her empty glass on the table, breaking off a chunk at the bottom.

"Who's she?" Rézia picks up the piece of glass and tosses it behind her.

"The wife of President Kennedy," Mariselle explains. "The President Kennedy that all the used clothes in Port-au-Prince are named after."

"Oh," Rézia says, now taking swigs directly from the rum bottle. "He was so handsome."

"She's pretty too," Mariselle says. "She spoke French. She lost her husband and two babies, yet she remained so beautiful. She made sadness beautiful."

Pushing the damaged glass aside, Mariselle describes her encounter with Jackie Kennedy. Jackie Kennedy's first husband, the president whom all the used clothes in Port-au-Prince are named after, had been dead for more than a decade when she came to Haiti. Her new husband was a Greek billionaire who'd had some business with our president. Mariselle's first sighting of Jackie Kennedy was on the pier at the Port-au-Prince harbor when Jackie Kennedy walked off an enormous yacht, wearing pink Bermuda shorts, a white T-shirt, a massive straw hat, and wide-rimmed sunglasses to guard her well-chiseled face. The wind almost blew her hat away. Almost blew her tiny body away, Mariselle recalled, but she held herself up and disembarked.

"My husband went to the pier to paint her portrait," Mariselle says, wiping the wet glass and bottle rings off the table with her palms. "He asked her what she wanted in her painting. She said in that whispery baby voice that she wanted the harbor behind her, the cargo ships and fishing boats and a few Haitian faces on the pier. So my husband painted her on the pier and put me in the background. If you ever come across that painting, somewhere between the Port-au-Prince harbor and Jackie Kennedy, you will see me."

WEEK 11

My mother used to say that we'll all have three deaths: the one when our breath leaves our bodies to rejoin the air, the one when we are put back in the earth, and the one that will erase us completely and no one will remember us at all. I sometimes hear a dog bark and I'm startled that it sounds a little like the dogs that roamed around me that day as I sat on the beach, watching my father's fishing boat being hauled ashore without him in it.

My father used to love cockfights. He enjoyed the way the men would gather in a circle and pass a bottle of rum from hand to hand as they watched. This showed that animals were much smarter than men, he used to say, the way so many of us would congregate to watch two small birds.

He went to dogfights too, but he never enjoyed them as much. He could never get the howl of a dying dog out of his head. At least cocks were small, he said; we eat them, after all.

WEEK 12

When I was a girl, I had a small notebook made of a few folded sheets held together by my mother's embroidering thread. There I sketched some figures, which were drawn so close together that they looked like they were fighting one another on the page.

My mother was the one who first thought they were fighting. She also thought they were frightening, so she made me a rag doll because she believed I was seeing these little shadows at night and was afraid of them.

Night after night, I clung to this rag doll, whose crooked eyes my mother had drawn over the white cloth with a piece of charcoal. After my father was gone, I twisted the doll's neck night after night. During the day, I crowded the pages in my notebook with more tiny faces, to keep me company in case my mother also disappeared.

WEEK 13

Even though I've sung at a lot of funerals, I'm not necessarily a religious person. But I agree to Rézia's idea to light candles so we can pass the real test.

Mariselle says we should pray to Saint Jude, the patron of lost causes. We add in there a prayer too, for our country.

"It's not a lost cause yet," Mariselle says, "because it made us."

To that we toast, forsaking our rum for Mariselle's Pinot Noir.

It feels like I'm drinking blood, not the symbolic blood of the sacraments, but real blood, velvet blood, our own blood.

I give them as keepsakes a few swatches of my mother's embroidery. Threads of red clouds, omens for good luck.

Then Rézia asks me, "Why didn't you go when you were asked to sing at the national palace?"

"Ordered," I correct her. "I was ordered to go sing there."

"Why didn't you go?" Rézia persists. "If you had gone, maybe you'd still be home."

I made a choice that I'd rather stop singing altogether than sing for the type of people who'd killed my father.

"Isn't it amazing?" Rézia says. "Jackie Kennedy can go to Haiti anytime she wants, but we can't."

WEEK 14

We won't know for some time if we passed. Yet Rézia's still shaking with post-test anxiety when we sit down, each of us with a bowl of leftover stew from the day's menu.

Mariselle is wearing a set of gold bangles that, when she moves her arms, sound like the type of miniature gourd rattles you might put on a child's grave.

"I finally unpacked my suitcases," she says, "to celebrate."

She's gotten a job at a gallery not far from Rézia's restaurant and will be selling paintings, some of them her husband's.

We celebrate with her by holding hands and twisting our way through the narrow spaces between the tables.

"And you, Freda, what are you going to do now?" an out-of-breath Mariselle asks when we stop.

"I'm going back," I say, sinking into a chair. "I'm going to join a militia and return to fight."

Both Mariselle and Rézia laugh so loud that it's all I can hear for some time. Not the fan twirling overhead or the trickle of rum and wine from bottle to glass.

"Look, it's the seventies," I protest. "Look at Fidel Castro. He had women with him."

They're still laughing, but also drinking. Laughing and drinking.

"It's not that." Mariselle is doubled over, clinging to her belly, chortling. "It's just that if you join a militia, we'll soon be reading about *you*."

"If you join a militia, you'll die." Rézia stops to wipe her damp forehead with her vetiver-scented hankie that now looks like a surrender flag. "Then who will sing at your funeral?"

The room is quiet now, except for the fan spinning overhead and a car horn blaring outside. Mariselle throws her head back, empties her entire glass in her mouth, then flings it across the room. We watch it fly, then land on the wall, breaking into a torrent of little pieces.

"Hey!" Rézia shuffles over with a broom and dustpan to

THE FUNERAL SINGER

pick up the shards. "Don't wreck my place. If I didn't have this place, I'd be as crazy as the two of you."

"We're not crazy." Mariselle tries to get up, but her knees buckle under her and she falls back in her chair.

"Freda, why don't you do it now?" Mariselle says. "Why don't you sing your own funeral song?"

"We'll help you," Rézia chimes in from where she's sweeping up glass across the room.

I clear my throat to show them that I can do it, am willing to do it, sing my own funeral song. Why not?

And that's how I begin my final performance as a funeral singer, or any kind of singer at all.

I sing "Brother Timonie." *Brother Timonie, Brother Timonie, we row on without you. But I'll know we'll meet again.*

Rézia and Mariselle catch on quickly and join in. We sing until our voices grow hoarse, sometimes making Brother Timonie a sister.

When we've exhausted poor Timonie, we move on to a few more songs, happier songs. And for the rest of the night we raise our glasses, broken and unbroken alike, to the terrible days behind us and the uncertain ones ahead.

THE DEW BREAKER

CIRCA 1967

1

He came to kill the preacher. So he arrived early, extra early, a whole two hours before the evening service would begin.

The sun had not yet set when he plowed his black DKW within a few inches of a row of vendors who had lined themselves along where he'd imagined the curb might be, to sell all kinds of things, from grilled peanuts to packs of cigarettes. He wanted a perfect view of the church entrance in case the opportunity came to do the job from inside his car without his having to get out and soil his shoes.

Catching the street merchants stealing glimpses at his elephantine frame, he shifted now and again to better fit between the car seat and the steering wheel, his wide belly spilling over his belt to touch the tip of the gearshift.

Later one of the women, who didn't want her name used, would tell the Human Rights people, "He looked like a pig in a calabash sitting there. Yes, I watched him. I watched him for a long time. I tried to frighten him with my old eyes. I belong to that church and I did not want to see my pastor die."

Rumors had been spreading for a while that the preacher had enemies in high places. His Baptist church was the largest in Bel-Air, one of the oldest and poorest communities in Haiti's capital, a neighborhood that one American journalist had described a few months earlier in a *Life* magazine article as "a hilly slum with an enviable view of the cobalt sea of Port-au-Prince harbor."

The church was called L'Eglise Baptiste des Anges, the Baptist Church of the Angels, which was printed in chalky letters on a clapboard sign over the front doors. Above the sign was a likeness of Jesus, scrawny, with a hollowed ivory face and two emaciated hands extended toward passersby.

The preacher had a radio show, which aired at seven every Sunday morning on Radio Lumière, so that those who could not visit his church could listen to his sermons before they went about their holy day. Rumors of the preacher's imminent encounter with the forces in power started as soon as he'd begun broadcasting his sermons on the radio the year before. Those at the presidential palace who monitored such things were at first annoyed, then enraged that the preacher was not sticking to the "The more you suffer on earth, the more glorious your heavenly reward" script. In his radio sermons, later elaborated on during midmorning services, the preacher called on the ghosts of brave men and women in the Bible who'd fought tyrants and nearly died. (He'd started adding women when his wife passed away six months before.) He exalted Queen Esther, who had intervened to halt a massacre of her people; Daniel, who had tamed lions intended to devour him; David, who had pebbled Goliath's defeat; and Jonah, who had risen out of the belly of a sea beast.

"And what will we do with *our* beast?" the preacher encouraged his followers to chant from beside their radios at home, as well as from the plain wooden pews of his sanctuary.

He liked to imagine the whole country screaming, "What will we do with our beast?" but instead it seemed as if everyone was walking around whispering the sanctioned national prayer, written by the president himself: "Our father who art in the national palace, hallowed be thy name. Thy will be done, in the capital, as it is in the provinces. Give us this day our new Haiti and forgive us our anti-patriotic thoughts, but do not forgive those anti-patriots who spit on our country and trespass against it. Let them succumb to the weight of their own venom. And deliver them not from evil."

The church members who were the most loyal of the radio listeners, when they were visited at home in the middle of the night and dragged away for questioning in the torture cells at the nearby Casernes Dessalines military barracks, would all bravely answer the same way when asked what they thought the preacher meant when he demanded, "What will we do with our beast?"

"We are Christians," they would say. "When we talk about a beast, we mean Satan, the devil."

The Human Rights people, when they gathered in hotel bars at the end of long days of secretly counting corpses and typing single-spaced reports, would write of the flock's devotion to the preacher, noting, *"Impossible to deepen that night.* These people don't have far to go to find their devils. Their devils aren't imagined; they're real."

Not all the church members agreed with the preacher's political line, however. Some would even tell you, "If the pastor continues like this, I leave the church. He should think about his life. He should think about our lives."

The light of day vanished as he waited, the street vendors exchanging places around him, day brokers going home to be replaced by evening merchants who sold fried meats, plantains, and more cigarettes, late into the night. Among the dusk travelers were his colleagues in their denim uniforms. He didn't know them intimately, but recognized a few. Those he did know loved to wear their uniforms, even though he didn't think they should on jobs like this. Not that there was anything subtle about this job. He was sure that even before the "uniforms" had arrived some of the neighborhood people, upon observing him, had already gone off to warn the preacher. He was equally certain that neither he nor his uniformed acquaintances would deter the preacher. From what he knew of the preacher's reputa-tion, he was certain that the preacher would come and the evening service would go on. For if he stayed home, it would mean the devil had won, the devil of his own fear.

The preacher didn't live far away. Four agents were even now in front of his modest two-room house, waiting to snatch him in case he tried to escape. Somehow he found it hard to imagine the preacher even being afraid. Perhaps he too was falling for the religious propaganda. The preacher would not be like the others, he told himself, who in the final hours before their arrests would plot impossible departures, run to trusted friends or relatives to parcel out their goods and their children.

In his work there were many approaches. Some of his colleagues tried to go as far from the neighborhoods where they grew up as possible when doing a task like this. Oth-ers relished returning to the people in their home areas, people who'd refused cough syrup for a mother or sister as she sat up the whole night coughing up blood. Some would rather "disappear" the schoolteachers who'd told them that they had heads like mules and would never learn to read or write. Others wanted to take revenge on the girls who were too self-important, who never smiled when their names were called out or when they were hissed at or whis-tled at in the street. Others still wanted to beat the girls' parents for asking their last names and judging their line-age not illustrious enough. But he liked to work on people he didn't know, people around whom he could create all sorts of evil tales.

For example, he could easily convince himself before killing the preacher that being Catholic, he wasn't supposed to like the Protestants anyway. They didn't dance. They made their women dress in white and cover their heads with matching handkerchiefs, scarves, or rags. They were always talking or singing about the devil, using biblical symbols that could easily be misinterpreted. So killing someone like the preacher wouldn't make him feel guilty for long, no matter where he had to do it.

In slaying the preacher, he could tell himself, he would actually be freeing an entire section of Bel-Air, men, women, and children who had been brainwashed with rites of incessant prayers and milky clothes. He'd be liberating them, he reasoned, from a Bible that had maligned them, pegged them as slaves, and told them to obey their masters, holy writings that he had completely vacated from his mind soon after the raucous party his parents had thrown to celebrate his first communion. With their preacher gone, the masses of Bel-Air would be more likely to turn back to their ancestral beliefs, he told himself, creeds carried over the ocean by forebears who had squirmed, wailed, and nearly suffocated in the hulls of Middle Passage kanntès, nègriers, slave ships.

The night before, the president of the republic had tried to send a painful message both to people like him and to people like the preacher. The president, often referred to as the Sovereign One, had been heard on the radio announcing the execution of nineteen young officers, members of the palace guard, who the president thought had betrayed him. The president, also known as the Renovator of the Fatherland, had listed the officers' names, roll-call style, on the radio, had answered "absent" for each of them, then had calmly announced, "They have been shot."

So now every order from the national palace was a loyalty test, a warning that worse things could come.

The preacher had already received his own warning. Six months before, the daughter of a rival pastor had been paid to slip a piece of poisoned candy to the preacher's wife during a women's auxiliary meeting. After his wife's death, the preacher had simply taken his wife's body to her village in the mountains to be buried in her family plot.

Considering the preacher's stubbornness made him tap his index finger on the .38 tucked away against his spine. It was a nervous habit, something he did whenever he caught himself thinking too much, too hard, for too long.

He had been constantly thinking about getting out of this life, moving to Florida, or even New York, making himself part of the new Haitian communities there, to keep an eye on the movements that were fueling the expatriate invasions at the borders. He could infiltrate the art galleries, makeshift coffee shops, where the exiled intellectuals were said to meet to drink coffee and rum and talk revolution. He was already saving up his money to begin a new life, carrying most of it with him in his back pocket but also keeping some in a cemented hole in his office at the barracks and the rest in a pouch in his mattress at home. But he couldn't leave until he followed his orders, proved his loyalty, and killed the preacher. Pushing all this to the back of his mind, he poked his head out of the car window and asked one of the boys who were studying in a group under the street lamp to get him a pack of cigarettes.

A childhood zinc deficiency had long ago removed his ability to taste things sweet or sour, hot peppers, confections, even the five-star rum he loved. So he ate things now for their smells and sounds rather than their taste, and he smoked potent cigarettes—Splendides, red.

He was not yet thirty years old, yet his voice was already too hoarse, his windpipe sometimes itching from a place he couldn't scratch. But he couldn't do without the smoke and the temporary cloudiness his cigars and cigarettes allowed him. No more than he could do without his five-star Barbancourt, one glass at a time over a game of cards, zo, or checkers with the smartest of the prisoners in the barracks.

Sometimes during his one-on-one "interviews," he would convince his captives that if they won the hazard games he commanded them to play, they could live, something that gave them a glint of hope unlike anything he'd ever seen in human eyes, except maybe during a fight when someone whose throat he had his hands around was suddenly on top of him squeezing, kicking, biting for life.

The night before, he'd dreamed he was leaving Haiti dressed as a nun after the government had fallen. Perhaps it was a sign from the gods, he told himself, warning him to retreat, and soon. He didn't want to wait until he was too old to leave. But when the order came about the preacher, he simply could not refuse.

The boy came back with the cigarettes and a withered copy of a history book tucked in his armpit. He pulled out a wad of cash as large as his own hand and let the boy have three gourdes of his change in honor of a past he couldn't deny.

His own parents were landowning peasants, who'd had him educated at a school run by Belgian priests, a school that was also attended by the children of the cane and vanilla plantation owners in the south, in Léogâne. His family had lost all their land soon after the Sovereign One had come to power in 1957, when a few local army officials decided they wanted to build summer homes there. Consequently his father had gone mad and his mother had simply disappeared. Rumor had it that she'd taken a boat to Jamaica with a neighbor who had been her first love but whom she had chosen not to marry because he'd had only one change of clothes, two pairs of secondhand shoes, no money, no house, no livestock, and no land. The man's lot had apparently improved even as his father's had deteriorated, and since the man had vanished at the same time as his mother, it seemed logical to believe that his mother had run off with him.

He had joined the Miliciens, the Volunteers for National Security, at nineteen, after his mother left. It began when the Volunteers came to his town bussing people to a presidential rally in the capital. They needed bodies to listen to one of the president's Flag Day speeches. People had wanted to go home for their hats and sunbonnets, but there was no time for that. Straw hats with fringed edges had been prepared for them with the president's name printed on them. There were many solemn faces on the camion that day, but his wasn't one of them. He was going to the city, where by raising his head and craning his neck he could see the president of his country.

En route to the capital that morning, he smoked his first pipe and drank three cups of homemade moonshine. One of the silent objectors who had been trying to numb himself before the rally had passed the pipe and kleren to him. With that first smoke and the public drinking of what he now considered inferior liquor, he felt himself transformed into an adult.

When he got to the city, he followed the throng of people to the vast, meticulously trimmed lawn of the national palace. He was mesmerized by the procession of humanity, standing before the whitest and biggest building in the whole country. Decorating the palace terraces were men with rifles, men dressed in uniforms with golden ropes like those he'd studied in pictures of the fathers of the independence in his own boyhood history book. And finally the president, slipping out onto the balcony dressed like a guardian of the cemetery in a black suit and coattails, a black hat, a .38 visibly attached to his belt, and a rifle at his side.

When he saw the president's ashen, spectacle-adorned

face, he decided he would never go back home. He finally believed his father's oft-repeated declaration that his son would never work the land, never carry a knapsack on his shoulders or a machete in his hand.

He listened for hours as the president read what seemed like a hundred-page book, in perfect nasal French. From the entire speech, he managed to retain only a few lines. If anyone tried to topple him, the president threatened, blood would flow in Haiti as never before. The land would burn from north to south, east to west. There would be no sunrise and no sunset, just one big flame licking the sky. He also remembered the tall tan woman in a teal dress at the president's side, the president's wife, fresh and buoyant as an azalea floating in a stream, staring uninterested down at the crowd. He had wondered if she had a handgun under her dress and wouldn't have been surprised if she did. He didn't move his head the whole time the president was speaking.

After the third, fourth, or fifth hour of the speech, he found himself dreaming. He thought he saw a flock of winged women circling above the palace dome, angry sibyls ranging in hue from cinnamon, honey, bronze, sable, to jet-black, hissing through the rest of the speech.

Later he would tell one of the many women he'd eventually take to bed, "I thought they were angels, caryatids, maybe a soul for each of us standing there in the sun."

And the woman would reply, "You can't afford to be a spiritual man."

· · ·

The boy was standing there not moving, even after he had given him the money. He pulled an additional five-gourdes bill from his pocket and handed it to the kid. He suddenly wanted to have some company, so he decided to engage the boy in conversation. There was a part of him that wished he could buy that child a future, buy all children like that a future. Perhaps not the future he would have himself, not the path his life would take, but another kind of destiny.

"What do you study?" he asked.

The boy replied, "History."

And he requested that the boy recite for him the lesson of the day. The boy stuttered and appeared nervous, as if recalling school punishments, rulers on the knuckles, harsh words from the teachers for not getting his lessons right.

He asked to see the boy's palms, for you could always tell how bright a student was, or how good he was at memorizing his lessons, by examining his palms and knuckles for ruler calluses and splinter marks.

The boy's hands were calloused indeed, but maybe it wasn't because he was dumb. Maybe it was because he didn't have the proper light in his house or because he had a book with missing pages or because he didn't get a chance to eat breakfast every morning.

He gave the boy yet another five gourdes and told him to go away. Too much was gathering in his head now around the kid's fate. He watched as the boy bought himself a pack of gum and two cigarettes, green Splendides, menthol. The boy inhaled deeply and exhaled with equal ability, forming a series of cloudy rings in the air. He then bought a handful of goat meat and fried plantains and shared them with five of his young friends, who were also milling around beneath the street lamp sharpening the tips of their pencils with razor blades as they recited their lessons to one another.

The boy would later tell a *Le Monde* journalist, "We saw him sit there all afternoon. I bought him cigarettes. With the money he gave me extra, I bought supper and candy and shared with my friends." But the boy would not mention the two loose cigarettes he had purchased for himself.

With the smoke clouding his lungs, he tried to forget about the boy by concentrating on his longing for a bottle of rum. He yearned for dominoes, a card game, sweet words, a bare thigh to run his hand up and down on, some close dancing, and a girl to polish his expensive belt buckle with the tip of her belly button. But all this would have to wait until the preacher was dead. And so he watched the boys suck the marrow out of the fried goat bones until the bones squeaked like whistles and clarinets and he thought of how hungry he'd been after the president's speech, when the crowd was left to find its own way home and when one of the many men in denim who were circling the palace that day had approached him and asked him whether he wanted to join the Miliciens, the Volunteers, what later would be called the macoutes. He had gotten an identification card, an indigo denim uniform, a homburg hat, a .38, and the privilege of marching in all the national holiday parades.

He didn't like the uniform. He thought it made him look like a dancer in a folklore show. And so he asked to wear regular clothes, eagerly provided for him when he appeared at the rich merchants' shops and showed his Volunteers membership card. His favorite line for them was, "I volunteered to protect national security. Unfortunately, or fortunately as you like, this includes your own."

With these words, restaurants fed him an enormous amount of food, which he ate eagerly several times a day because he enjoyed watching his body grow wider and meatier just as his sense of power did. A doctor, his landlord, gave him two rooms on the lower floor of a two-story house for free. Bourgeois married women slept with him on the cash-filled mattress on his bedroom floor. Virgins of all castes came and went as well. And the people who had looked down on him and his family in the past, well, now they came all the way from Léogâne to ask him for favors.

Dressed in their best city outfits, they arrived at the dark little office he closed off for himself in one of the back cells at the military barracks and called him "Sergeant," "Colonel," "General." Some even blasphemously ennobled him "Little President."

"It's been ten days," they would say, "since my son was taken."

"My daughter is gone," they'd sob. "And I know it was not of her will."

Whenever he wanted to, he could solve their problems by simply writing a note to the Léogâne chiefs, who, because he was located in the capital and could read and write, deemed his position above their own.

He made a few trips a month to Léogâne, to visit his father, whose insanity manifested itself in his walking naked to the marketplace twice a week, clutching a rock in each fist.

Once when he was in Léogâne, he went and talked to each of the officials who'd taken over his father's land. He told them all, "We're all the same now, but I'll never forget what you did to my parents. Now I'm the one everyone comes to in the capital. A closed mouth doesn't catch flies, so I won't say any more. But watch yourself."

It was a simple monologue that, even though it didn't get him back all their land, regained his father the house where both he and the father were born and stopped the requests for favors from the hometown for a while.

The way he acted at the inquisitions in his own private cell at Casernes eventually earned him a lofty reputation among his peers. He was the one who came up with the most physically and psychologically taxing trials for the prisoners in his block. He was suffering, he knew it now, from what one of his most famous victims, the novelist Jacques Alexis, had written was the greatest hazard of the job. Tu deviens un véritable gendarme, un bourreau. It was becoming like any other job. He liked questioning the prisoners, teaching them to play zo and bezik, stapling clothespins to their ears as they lost and removing them as he let them win, convincing them that their false victories would save their lives. He liked to paddle them with braided cowhide, stand on their cracking backs and jump up and down like a drunk on a trampoline, pound a rock on the protruding bone behind their earlobes until they couldn't hear the orders he was shouting at them, tie blocks of concrete to the end of sisal ropes and balance them off their testicles if they were men or their breasts if they were women.

When one of the women who had been his prisoner at Casernes was interviewed three decades later for a documentary film in her tiny restaurant in Miami's Little Haiti neighborhood, the gaunt, stoop-shouldered octogenarian, it was said, would stammer for an hour before finally managing to speak, pausing for a breath between each word. She couldn't remember his name, nor could she even imagine what he might look like these days, yet she swore she could never get him out of her head.

"I know they say 'the fish don't see the water,' " she would say, "but this one, he saw the water fine. He used to call me by my name. He'd lean close to my ears to tell me, 'Valia, I truly hate to unwoman you. Valia, don't let me unwoman you. Valia, tell me where your husband is and I won't cut out your . . . I can't even say it the way he said it.

I refuse to say it the way he did. He'd wound you, then try to soothe you with words, then he'd wound you again. He thought he was God."

2

"I know my God and I'm placing myself in His hands," the preacher said as he devoured his supper of four squares of pulpy bread and a steaming cup of ginger tea. The preacher was dressed in his best cream jacket and vest ensemble, one he usually wore on Sundays with a striped red and ocher tie.

The preacher was a dapper man, graceful and elegant, in spite of his disproportionately long limbs, which appeared slightly unbalanced with the rest of his body.

At his long mahogany table, which he'd designed and built himself for meals with church members, the preacher was surrounded by three of his deacons, who were trying to convince him to cancel the evening service and stay home.

"Let the people come to you tonight," suggested the senior deacon, a house builder who'd known the preacher since they were both fourteen years old.

"We can have the service here in the house," chimed in one of the younger deacons, Lionel Noël, the third being his brother, Joël Noël.

Ever since he'd begun broadcasting his radio show and had lost his wife, perhaps as a result of what he said on the air, the preacher had grown accustomed to these displays of fearful affection and had hence learned that the best way to appease them was to maintain his calm, while citing Bible passages, almost as incantations to soothe those who thought they could save his life.

What they didn't realize, or didn't want to acknowledge, was that he'd already decided to give his life, had made a pact with Heaven to be sacrificed for his country. Besides, there was no point in running or hiding. If the people in power truly wanted to find him, they could. They could enter his house and drag him away, from his bath, from his supper table, from his bed. They could find someone to poison him just as they had his wife.

The night before, nineteen members of the palace guard had had their executions announced on the radio by the president himself. If this could happen to former allies of the government, how much harder could it be to capture and kill him?

He'd dreamed his own death so many times that he was no longer afraid of it. He'd imagined himself being pushed off the highest mountain peak in Port-au-Prince, forced to drink a gallon of bleach, burned at the stake like Joan of Arc, beheaded like John the Baptist. In all of his dreams, however, he always saw himself being resurrected. When he was thrown off the top of Mòn Lopital, he sprouted wings and soared to the clouds. When he was made to drink a gallon of bleach, it went through his body like water and forced itself out through his urine. When he was bound to firewood, sprinkled with kindling and gasoline, and set on fire, the flames burned through the ropes that bound his wrists and ankles, the smoke blinded his enemies, and he strolled past them without being seen. When he was decapitated like John the Baptist, he bent down to the floor, picked up his own head, and fitted it back on as though he were a plastic doll.

That night at the supper table, just as he had during every other difficult moment in his life—including when he was just a boy and had lost his young brother in the sea and when his wife had died a few months before—he reminded himself of his own personal creed, that life was neither something you defended by hiding nor surrendered calmly on other people's terms, but something you lived bravely, out in the open, and that if you had to lose it, you should also lose it on your own terms.

Rising from his chair, he picked up his Bible, a leather-bound monogrammed volume, and thumped it against his palm as if to pound away his last shreds of doubt about going into the night.

"It's time for the service," he said to the deacons, while stroking the front cover. "I don't think you three should walk with me to the church tonight. I'll walk alone."

The senior deacon stretched his body upward, extending his right hand toward the preacher's face. For a brief second the preacher thought his friend was going to slap him, or perhaps signal to the sons, the preacher's godchildren, to grab and bind him, but all the elder did was remove an errant black string from the preacher's shoulder. Still, finding the string seemed like a slight ploy, something to delay them, to earn one more minute, to keep him inside the house a bit longer.

The preacher tapped the Bible against the elder deacon's lowered arm, signaling him and his sons to remove themselves from his path.

When it seemed like there was nothing else to do, the deacons stepped aside and allowed him to walk through the doorway. Once the preacher had carefully padlocked his front door, the three men reluctantly followed him across the shaky wooden bridge over the narrow rain canal that separated his house from the unpaved street.

As usual, Rue Tirremasse was muggy, dusty, and loud, and seemed much brighter than it should have with only one distant street lamp in sight. The preacher waved to his neighbor across the street, an old man who sold cassava bread bathed in homemade peanut butter from a stall in front of his house.

A konpa song praising the government (*you have led us/you have fed us* was the chorus) blared from the makeshift barbershop operating out of someone's living room in the house next to the old man's. Two young men were sitting inside playing cards as a boy's head was shaved of hair and lice. The preacher waved to the barber and the men, who waved back. Could they be his executioners? The ones he'd been told would be waiting out on the street for him?

A woman selling grilled corn in front of the barbershop called out to the preacher, "How are we tonight, Pastor?"

Just as he always did whenever she greeted him that

way, he nodded that he was fine, but this time took the extra step of bowing in her direction.

The preacher then spotted a young couple he'd married. They had notebooks pressed against their chests as they walked toward him. The wife was taking a secretarial course, while the husband was studying to be an accountant. Their parents had rushed to have the preacher marry them when the girl became pregnant, but she'd suffered a miscarriage soon after the wedding.

"How are you, Pastor?" she asked when they stopped to greet him.

"How are the courses coming?" the preacher asked.

"They're very difficult, Pastor," the young husband answered. "We have a lot of studying to do. This is why you haven't seen us at the weekday services."

The three deacons were still following closely behind the preacher. They were a bit more comfortable now, feeling protected by the geniality of each of the preacher's encounters. They too participated in the greetings, nodding and waving hello.

A widow whom the preacher occasionally hired to wash and iron his clothes stopped him to ask when she should come by for the next batch.

"Pastor, you're not kind," she said. "You wear the same clothes all the time so you won't give me the work."

The preacher laughed before moving on to the house of a shoeshine man, who, when he wasn't shining shoes, always sat in a low chair in his doorway watching the

street. The shoeshine man was one of many who'd con-
spired to empty slop jars from their roofs over the heads
of some Volunteers who'd come to arrest a group of phi-
losophy students who'd performed Samuel Beckett's *En
Attendant Godot* at the nearby student center.

"*We are all born mad.*" The preacher now recalled that particular line from the play. "*Some remain so.*"

The Volunteers had shot at all the surrounding houses
the night after the play was performed, but thankfully no
one had been hurt.

"Pastor, your shoes look a little dusty tonight." The
shoeshine man reached under his chair and pulled out his
shine toolbox.

"Léon, there's no need to have polished shoes at night,"
the preacher said.

"Pastor, a man like you should always have clean shoes,"
Léon argued.

"They won't stay clean for long," the preacher said.

"Pastor, before you can say Amen, I will be done."

"Maybe tomorrow, Léon," said the preacher.

The "tomorrow" made the shoeshine man smile. The
deacons smiled also, finding further reason to hope.

The men were almost at the church when they reached
the one street lamp on their stretch of Rue Tirremasse.
A group of boys was gathered there in the direct path
of the light beam. Some of the boys were singsonging
their school lessons to one another, while others studied
alone, pacing back and forth with their heads bowed. The

preacher made out one of the boys who faithfully attended Sunday school with his mother, a ten-year-old who despite the mother's scoldings was not above begging from the vendors and passersby. The boy had a cigarette butt in his hand. When he spotted the preacher, he threw the butt on the ground and darted down a dark alley away from the street.

On another occasion the preacher might have remarked to the deacons for their own information, "Do you see that? Do you see what Satan's doing to our youth, our jeunesse étudiante?" However, as he approached the gates of his church and looked up to greet the image of the Christ with the pale arms extended toward him, his mind was less on the flock than the wolves who though he hadn't noticed them were certainly looming.

Inside, the preacher flipped a light switch. The dangling bulbs flickered from high in the middle of the room. As the preacher strolled casually to the altar, the deacons brought out the kerosene lamps they always had on reserve in case there was a blackout, the collection baskets they passed at every service for offerings, and a gallon of water that they parceled out in a glass to the preacher to refresh his voice during the service.

The service went on as usual that night, but many of the members who usually came didn't attend. A few new faces were spotted in the congregation, however—people who had wandered in off the street to rest a few minutes on their way somewhere else, others like Léon who weren't

religious but had heard about the militia men milling
about and thought they might be of help to the preacher
should an ambush be attempted against him.

Throughout the service, which ran longer than the usual
hour, the preacher sang with all his might; he swayed his
body back and forth, pounded his fists on the pulpit,
stamped his feet, jumped up in the air and back, and
dashed up to each pew to encourage the congregants to
join them.

His sermon that night was more like a testimony. It was
a remembrance of the day of his wife's death.

He would always remember her eyes, he said. There
was something about them that wasn't quite right that
afternoon. Maybe it was the way the tear ducts kept filling
up and drying up again, with the tears never spilling down
her face. Or maybe it was the way her pupils were so
enlarged that they became one with her irises. Or maybe
it was the way she kept fighting to keep the upper and
lower lids apart, as though it was the greatest battle of her
life. In any case, it was obvious as soon as she staggered
home and slipped into bed that she was going to die.

Her limbs were all moving slowly but separately, as
though they were no longer controlled by the rest of her
body. She had already lost her power to speak, her ability
to answer when he called her name, begging her to tell
him what was wrong. Her lips moved, but no sounds came
out of them. Still, he did his best to follow their laggard
course to get some idea, some clue as to what she wanted
him to do.

He screamed for a neighbor to run and get his friend, the elder deacon, the one with the car. They would take her to the General Hospital on the chance that the doctors could do something to save her.

In all the confusion, he had forgotten to pray. Maybe his prayers could have brought her back. Even though her body was growing colder, she was not yet dead.

By the time the neighbor returned with the elder deacon, his wife was no longer breathing. She had let out one final sigh right before they'd walked through the front door. He would always remember that sigh, dislodged almost out of frustration, as if to say, Why don't you hear me? Why don't you understand me? Why can't you save me? He had wondered then if his wife's death had had anything to do with the women's auxiliary meeting that she'd just attended, a meeting called by a fellow pastor's daughter, a girl who'd shown no interest in religion before but who was all of a sudden saying that she wanted to know God.

The autopsy showed that his wife had been poisoned, something fast and deadly that the General Hospital coroner couldn't, or wouldn't, identify. He'd felt some sense of vindication when the girl who might have poisoned his wife had disappeared, reportedly arrested and confined to the torturous dungeons of Fort Dimanche prison for some other crime. But he could never shake from his thoughts the notion that his wife's death had been his fault, that she'd been killed to punish him for the things he said on his radio program or from the pulpit of his church.

So he was now publicly begging his dead wife's forgiveness. He was hoping she would hear him from Heaven and absolve him.

A few of the faithful in the congregation, those who thought they knew the preacher well, including the Noël deacons, shifted in their seats, looking sad and puzzled but mostly fearful for the preacher and for themselves. They were glad that the preacher was finally showing some sign of grief and hinting that he might change his ways, back down from his verbal attacks on the government, but they worried that this was the wrong way to do it, on a night when anything that came out of his mouth might further enrage his enemies.

A group of women got up and quickly walked out. Those passersby who'd simply stopped in to rest filed out behind them, not quite understanding what was going on but sensing somehow that it could lead to trouble, that they might be fingered as anti-patriots merely for listening to what was being said.

Léon, the shoeshine man, wiped a tear from his eye, remembering his own son who was one of those men who roamed the night in denim uniforms and carried people away to their deaths. His son might have been one of those he'd emptied the slop jars on and who had shot in his direction in return, for a good Volunteer, it was said, should be able to kill his mother and father for the regime.

Even though Léon hated what his son did, he still had to let his boy come home now and then for the boy's mother's sake and still had to acknowledge that maybe it was because of his boy that he'd not yet been arrested.

The preacher continued talking about his wife, remembering how her lips were so memorable, bright pink against her very dark face, how the space between her mouth and nose was cupped, shaped like a seashell, how the tip of her nostrils seemed to dip into the shell whenever she smiled, and how he'd done his best that day to try and make her smile, just to see that one last time.

He had loved his wife as soon as he saw her—his voice was growing hoarse and tired—he'd had no family in the city when he came to her father's church at fourteen. He said as much to her when he met her at the first service he attended in this church, and she insisted that her parents take him in.

He converted from Catholicism so he could sit in this church with her, becoming a minister so her parents—he was so glad that she was now with them in Heaven—he became a minister so her parents would let him marry her.

He was still speaking out his reverie when his stepsister Anne walked in and out of the congregation within seconds. Anne was returning from her first cosmetology class. He'd signed her up that morning, her third in the city. He could tell from the cool, distant look on her face that she knew nothing of the immediate threat, the killers lurking about, his possible arrest. His sister—for his father and

her mother had ordered them to always call each other
frè, sè, "brother," "sister"—had remained in their home village until a few days ago. In the seventy-two hours she'd
been with him, however, he'd told and retold her of the
day of his wife's death and now it was too much. She was
angry, angry at him for spending so much of his time and
energy on the people in government, tired of his delusions
to one day unseat them and set the masses free when he'd
simply walked away from his own family, his old life, the
place where the brother, with whom she shared a mother
and he a father, had drowned. She would now go to his
house and wait for him, to tell him all this once he
returned. Besides, she was hungry and wanted to get
something to eat.

His sister's quick appearance and departure did not
break the preacher's flow of reminiscences, however. A
half hour later, as the preacher was still recounting the sad
tale of his wife's death, a fat man, whose very large head
was crowned with a deep widow's peak, burst through the
church's front door. Behind the fat man was a group of
Volunteers, all dressed in denim uniforms and wearing
dark glasses whose front surfaces were like mirrors, dis-
torting the room into curvatures and the churchgoers
into miniatures. The men waved their handguns and rifles
at the congregation and told them to keep their heads
down, their foreheads pressed against the pews in front of
them. The fat man wobbled down the aisle toward the
preacher, held a .38 in one hand and with the other
grabbed the preacher's neck, wrapping his long, plump

fingers around the preacher's Adam's apple, putting extra pressure on the preacher's voice box to keep him from speaking. The extra force was not necessary, for the preacher had spent months preparing himself for a moment such as this, imagining what he would or would not do in this exact situation, and now that the moment had come, he was glad that his body was cooperating, no unexpected pulmonary attacks, no sudden bowel movements.

A few of the Volunteers joined the fat man and the preacher at the altar. Two of them grabbed the preacher's arms and swung them around behind his back and held them there. The preacher winced in pain only once as the fat man and the others shoved him toward the front door.

The street outside the church was suddenly empty, all the merchants and children gone, all doors padlocked, with no light streaming out.

The preacher imagined his neighbors trembling in their hiding places, wondering if they would be visited next. But tonight, it seemed, was his night, and his alone.

The preacher was thrown in the back of a truck. A group of Miliciens piled on top of him. He raised his feet close to his chest as they shoved him from side to side, pounding rifle butts on random parts of his body. His face was now pressed against the metal undulations of the truck bed, boot soles and heels raining down on him, cigarette butts being put out in his hair, which sizzled and popped like tiny grains of rock salt in an open fire. He was hit with jolts of shock from what felt like portable electric devices pressed against the heels of his now bare feet.

He welcomed the sudden jerk of the truck taking off to race down the empty streets, because it provided a brief interruption of the assaults. He felt a flurry of hands sweep over his face. Some raised his head, and for a moment he caught a glimpse of the unfamiliar faces surrounding him, many now with the dark glasses off.

A dusty black rag was wrapped around his eyes, then tied in rigid knots around the back of his head. Now that his eyes were covered, he craved to see.

The truck suddenly stopped. The men nearest to him exchanged a few words with the people in a car up front. It seemed to him that the conversation was about where to take him, the nearby military barracks or the prison, Casernes or Fort Dimanche. It was said that if one went to the former there was a small chance of coming out alive, but the latter was literally a sepulcher from which no one was ever expected to resurface.

He thought he heard Casernes, the barracks. The truck was off again, and the blows resumed for the rest of his journey. He lost track of his own movements, his body cringing at every strike.

The truck stopped once more, and he felt the truck bed slowly rise as the Miliciens jumped off.

He heard a woman scream, "Jean! Jean! Is that you?" And if his name had been Jean, he would have thought himself already dead, being called forward by his wife from the other side.

He tried for the first time to loosen his hand and foot restraints so that he could perhaps move closer to the empty space where the woman's voice was coming from.

A shot was fired somewhere. In the air? At him? At the woman calling Jean? He didn't feel the expected hot burst of flames anywhere on his skin. Someone dragged him by the legs, pulled him forward, removing his jacket, and then he felt himself falling from the back of the truck onto the concrete. He fell on his face, crushing his forehead. His blood quickly soaked the blindfold, a warm veil of red covering the darkness over his eyes. He was being dragged by the legs over the rise of a curb. With each yank forward, a little bit of him was bruised, peeled away. He felt as though he was shedding skin, shedding voice, shedding sight, shedding everything he'd tried so hard to make himself into, a well-dressed man, a well-spoken man, a well-read man. He was leaving all that behind now with bits of his flesh in the ground, morsel by morsel being scraped off by pebbles, rocks, tiny bottle shards, and cracks in the concrete.

He tried to make himself as limp as possible as he was pushed down some uneven steps that at different moments in his descent wedged themselves between his ribs.

He was probably in a cell now, for he heard the rattling of bars and a lock being turned. He heard some breathing, some of it labored, and loud, moaning men. The smell of rotting flesh made him want to sneeze. There were some shadows circling him, sniffing like rats following the scent of blood. His head was spinning like a child's top. The shadows were spinning too and then faded all together.

He was disappointed to find himself awakened again sometime in the night. A warm liquid was trickling down on his face and when he opened his mouth to quench his thirst with it, he realized it was urine.

Ave urina! The ridiculous thought entered his mind from some source he couldn't quite recall. Morituri te salutant, I who am about die salute you.

His blindfold was now gone, but his inflamed eyelids formed a cover of their own. He fell into his darkness once more, this time even more abruptly than before.

3

The lights suddenly went out in the house and all over Rue Tirremasse, just as Anne was feeling one of those odd sensations she'd been experiencing since childhood. Even though it was pitch-black, she felt a slight pinch in both her eyes, another curtain of darkness settling in, further deepening the obscurity around her. Her face was growing progressively warmer, as though the candle she now so longed to light had already been ignited beneath the skin on her cheekbones. A high-pitched sound was ringing in her ears, like a monotonic flute, just as her nose was being bombarded with the sweet, lingering smell of frangipanis in bloom. Anticipating the convulsions to follow, she lowered herself to the ground and lay on her back, spreading her arms and legs apart. She imagined observing herself from somewhere high above, perhaps perched from the ceiling, watching herself on the cool cement floor, looking like a butterfly whose wings had been fractured, forcing it to set down and slowly die. Her breathing was shallow, the pauses growing longer between each cycle. Her body stiffened and the inside of her mouth felt crowded, her tongue swelling and spreading out over her teeth, filling them with the briny taste of dirty seawater. Fragmented moments from her life were filing past her, event after event streaming by at high speed on the giant puppet screen she now imagined her mind to be: her younger brother's drowning, her stepbrother's departure from their seaside village, perhaps to avoid the waters that had taken their brother's life, their respective parents' death from either chagrin or hunger or both, her recent move to the city to join her older brother, his inability to stop speaking about his wife's death, which, it seemed, was not so unlike this death she was sure she was experiencing.

Maybe she shouldn't have left the church a few moments ago. He was going on again about his wife and she was tired of it. Based on her brother's own accounts, she couldn't help but blame him for his wife's death. What made him think he could denounce the powerful on the radio, of all places, and not risk the safety of those he loved? She wanted to tell him these things, hoped she would get the chance. Yet there she was, dying again or possessed again, she couldn't tell which. If she were possessed, then why did the spirits wait until she was alone to enter her body, mount her the way she'd mounted docile

horses as a child? There was no one there to hear whatever revelations the spirits would communicate through
her, and when she came around again, if she came around
again, she would have no recollection of this semi-mortal
trance, except perhaps the sudden certainty that even as
she was lying there, somewhere her older brother too was
failing. Either his body itself was dying or something
inside him was dying, but she feared that she might never
see him again.

4

He was told to release the preacher. The change of orders
had come directly from the national palace. He had
missed an important nuance; the preacher had been *arrested*
rather than *killed*. The arrest had been sloppily handled.

It was supposed to be a quiet operation, his superior,
Rosalie, a short, stout, bespectacled woman, told him. She
was in her fifties and one of the few high-ranking women
in the barracks. Somehow she had become a friend, even
though he didn't see her often. She was frequently at the
palace, where she had direct access to the president, for
whom she was trying to recruit more female volunteers.
Like the president, she had a deep love for folklore, which
according to her they discussed frequently. And since the
president had named his volunteer militia after the mythic
figure of the Tonton Macoute, a bogeyman who abducted
naughty children at night and put them in his knapsack,
she wanted to name her female force Fillette Lalo, after a

rhyme most of the country grew up singing, a parable about a woman who eats children.

When she'd shared all this with him, over glasses of rum and Cuban cigars, she even sang the rhyme, as if he needed to be reminded of it.

> *Little Bird, where are you going?*
> *I am going to Fillette Lalo's.*
> *Fillette Lalo eats little children.*
> *If you go, she will eat you too.*
> *Brikolobrik*
> *Brikolobrik*
> *Hummingbirds eat soursop.*

For others, the song recital might have seemed menacing, like a blatant effort to cast herself as the hummingbird to his soursop, but not for him. She had taken him under her wing, seeing in him some of her own zeal for the job. But now she wasn't singing or laughing. She was angry.

"By all accounts, the arrest turned into a cockfight," she said. She had long tried to copy the nasal inflection of her boss, the president, coming up with her own variation of it. "You went into a church filled with people when you could have gotten him on the street. Why did you bring him here?"

There were too many people milling around outside the church, he wanted to say, including that damned boy. He hadn't been able to get a clear shot. He thought he could do the job better right here, in the barracks.

"You wanted him to suffer," Rosalie was saying, smirking almost as if in admiration. "You took too many liberties. You disobeyed."

He had failed her, and himself. Now the palace wanted the preacher released. They wanted the preacher sent out into the night, fearful and powerless, wondering when he would see them next. They didn't want him to become some kind of martyr.

"He's your responsibility," she told him, turning on her heel, as if for a military-style about-face. "I've seen him and he looks very bad. Under no circumstances should he die here."

He called out to one of the many low-level Volunteers who were always waiting in the prison's narrow corridors for the next order. "Bring the preacherman in," he said.

As the Volunteer disappeared from the doorway, he felt the usual tightening in his throat. It was something he always faced in the few moments before confronting a prisoner. Would the prisoner be fearful, bold? Would he/she put up a fight?

He was not anticipating a struggle. He wouldn't try the usual methods on the preacher. He would simply encourage the preacher to abandon his activities, then tell him to go home.

5

"Hey, preacherman!" a voice was calling from outside the dark cell. "Come on over here!"

The preacher had no idea where "here" was. The Voice would have to keep shouting if it wanted him to find it. The preacher was half sitting, half squatting, with his back against a clammy wall. He was surrounded by the half dozen prisoners who had pissed on him. Others were curled on the filthy floor, sleeping. The ones who had pissed on him were exchanging a few words. From their garbled conversations, he gathered that they'd performed a kind of ritual cure. They believed that their urine could help seal the open wounds on his face and body and keep his bones from feeling as though they were breaking apart and melting under his skin. When the prisoners who'd pissed on him heard the Voice calling from outside the cell, they quickly parted around him, leaving the preacher a blurred view of a single shadow peering in through the rusting cell bars.

"You," the Voice called out to the others inside the cell. "Bring the new prisoner here."

Once again the preacher felt the agonizing sensation of many hands grabbing him at once, then carrying him from the back to the front of the cell. His head was still spinning, but somehow he managed to make his feet touch the ground, even as he was being held up high by his armpits. When he reached the bars at the front of the cell, he grabbed them and held on tightly. The men who were holding him up must have felt his unexpected surge of strength; they released him and left him standing on his own.

The Voice was now only a few inches from the preacher's face. It broke into a halting laugh.

"You're a lucky man," it was saying. "This is your lucky day, you lucky man."

The metal bars slid open, displacing his grip on them; then the shadow grabbed him and slammed him against the outside wall. He couldn't tell how many people were there, in the cell or in the cramped corridor between the wall and the cell. His body crumpled, his legs buckling under him as he slipped to the slimy foul-smelling ground.

The Voice ordered him to get up and follow it down the corridor. Was he moving or were the walls, caked with blood and fecal stains, moving on their own?

"Hurry up or I'll leave you here," the Voice said.

The preacher didn't want to be left there, squatting in the squalid limbo between freedom and imprisonment, between life and death. He thought of his wife and his sister, imagining himself moving closer to one and farther away from the other. His sister would survive without him, he told himself. She was strong; she had always known how to do for herself. She had her faith, no matter that unlike him she'd remained a Catholic. She also had his house, which she could sell if she needed money. She'd just begun that cosmetology course. Once she was done with her course, she could work as a beautician or open a shop. The only thing that worried him as far as she was concerned was her epilepsy. Even when she was a child, she never seemed to accept or understand that she was epileptic, coming up with all sorts of mystical reasons for her seizures, everything but the disease itself. He hoped she would never choose to have children. She'd had one of her seizures at the beach while watching their young brother and had let him drown. It's possible that his wife had also had epilepsy, had died from it. But he couldn't be distracted by these things now. The Voice was slipping away from him. He had to focus, concentrate all the strength he had left on his legs. Using the wall to support his weight, he climbed onto his feet and followed.

There was light waiting for him at the end of the corridor, all of it spilling out from one room, which he assumed was his destination. He could see a little better now. Maybe the urine cures had helped.

Dozens of eyes were peering at him from behind the cell bars on either side of the corridor. Some of the prisoners whispered, "Bonne chance." They also thought him lucky. He was going to be released or he was going to die. Either way, he was going to be free.

6

Anne loved miracles, read about them whenever she could, listened to religious radio stations for testimonies of manifestations of the miraculous in everyday life. Her reawakening was a miracle. Once again she had returned from the dead. Her body was aching from whatever contortions the spirits had put it through, but she was back now and she wasn't alone. The shoeshine man, Léon, was standing over her, holding a kerosene lamp while peering down at her on the ground. He helped her onto a chair and asked if she was all right. She nodded.

He had bad news, he said. Her brother had been arrested at the church. It seemed like an army had come for him. It didn't look good. He'd learned that they'd taken him to Casernes.

She had seen Casernes, the mustard-colored building that looked like a warship, anchored in the middle of downtown Port-au-Prince. They'd walked past it that same morning when he had taken her to enroll for her course. The cemetery was not too far away.

She didn't take long in deciding to go.

"Excuse me, Léon," she said. "I can't stay here."

He handed her a cup of water. She sipped some of the water, used the rest to wet her face, then got up, walked past him, and sprinted out the door. He ran after her, but could not keep up.

When she looked back, she saw him standing in the middle of the empty street, holding the lamp up with one hand while trying to motion for her to come back with the other. Standing there, he looked like both the angel of life and the angel of death, she thought as she continued running.

7

The death chamber was not what the preacher was expecting. He thought he would see all kinds of animate and inanimate contraptions, from killer dogs and voracious snakes to crosses to nail the prisoners side by side, heavy river rocks to grind their skulls, ice picks, clubs and knuckle-dusters, guillotines and syringes for lethal injections. The preacher was frankly disappointed when he staggered into the nine-by-twelve-foot mustard-colored prison office and forced his bloody, swollen eyes farther apart only to find the same large man who had taken him from the church sitting behind an old desk that took up half the room and the blurry vision of a single lightbulb dangling directly above the fat man's head. The room was hot and foul-smelling with the stench of body fluids mixed with tobacco. The Voice shoved the preacher toward the fat man's desk, which the preacher nearly toppled onto.

The fat man asked the Voice to bring in a chair and the Voice rushed out and came back with a low sisal chair the size of a child's rocker, the kind of chair the peasants called a "gossiping" chair because it made it so easy to squat and chat. The chair was much lower than the fat man's desk, and it was obvious that the height and size of the chair were meant to make the preacher feel smaller than the fat man, who was a whole lot larger than most people anyway.

The preacher decided to squeeze himself into the chair, which squeaked and swayed unsteadily beneath him. The fat man signaled for the Voice to leave the room and the Voice did so immediately. Even though the wobbly metal mustard door was still open, the size of the room made the preacher feel as though it had been suddenly sealed shut.

The fat man got up from behind his desk and strolled to

the preacher's side. From the preacher's angle, the fat man seemed quite massive, like some kind of ambulant mountain on giant feet.

"Listen, I'm going to tell you something," the fat man began in a rather slow, scratchy voice. To the preacher's wounded, much-pounded-on ears, it sounded as though the fat man was speaking from inside a bucket. "All I want to tell you is that you must stop what you've been doing."

The preacher was feeling restrained in the little chair as if he were chained to it. The tiny bloodsucking pinèz bugs, which inhabited such chairs, were already digging through his now torn and filthy pants, mining his buttocks for their nourishment. The preacher didn't dare move or scratch himself. Obviously the fat man had some childish game in mind for him. The fat man was going to give him hope and then take it away. He would be questioned, then returned to his cell to wait for his execution or for the next inquisition, which would be even more brutal than his capture.

The fat man was moving closer to him, extending his hefty hand as if to help him out of the small chair. This was probably one of the subtle torture methods the fat man used, reasoned the preacher. He made you uncomfortable, then pretended to relieve your discomfort so you'd feel grateful to him and think he was on your side.

As the fat man leaned in, the preacher began to shake. He didn't want to appear afraid, but he was. He had been counting on a quick death, not one where he would disappear in stages of prolonged suffering interrupted by a few seconds of relief. He had never thought he'd have reason to hope that maybe his life might be spared. He hadn't expected the kindness of his cellmates, men of different skin tones and social classes all thrown together in this living hell and helping one another survive it.

From their skeletal frames and festering sores, he could tell that some of them had been there for a long time, waiting, plotting, and dreaming of their release. Many of them were forgotten by the world outside, given up for dead. For indeed they had died. They were being destroyed piece by piece, day by day, disappearing like the flesh from their bones. He didn't want to die like that, stooped in a filthy corner of the cell with parasites burrowed in his flesh.

Still the fat man's face kept moving closer to his and the fat hand was still extended, offering to grab him out of the chair. For what? To take him to the real torture chamber? The one he'd always imagined?

The preacher pushed his body back, moving away from the fat man's hand. The chair squeaked underneath him and crashed, breaking the wooden legs into several pieces and dropping him on the floor. The fat man was still leaning down to him, his hand still extended. Now the hand seemed compelling, urgent, for he needed it to get off the ground. He was going to reach for it when he noticed the fat man smiling, his giant face growing wider with his cheeks spread apart.

The preacher wanted to cry, but he couldn't. He couldn't let the devil see him weep, so he lowered his head and pushed his arms behind him to balance himself on the floor.

His hand landed on one of the chair's broken pieces. He ran his fingers over the ragged edge, which sloped upward toward a sharp tip. He grabbed the piece of wood and aimed. He wanted to strike the fat man's eyes, but instead the spiked stub ended up in the fat man's right cheek and sank in an inch or so.

The fat man's shock worked in his favor, for it allowed him a few seconds to slide the piece of wood down the fat man's face, tearing the skin down to his jawline.

The fat man snatched the preacher's wrist and pressed down on it hard, almost stopping the blood flow to his fingers. The piece of wood slipped from the preacher's hand, falling on his lap. The fat man grabbed the preacher by the shoulders and slammed his body against the concrete. The space was small, leaving the preacher little room to budge. The fat man checked his face with his hands even as the blood was dripping down his neck onto the front of his shirt. He pulled out his gun, the same .38 he'd waved at the congregation at the church, and fired.

The preacher knew that as soon as the burst of light that had left the fat man's gun landed on his body, it would be over. Were he to come back, he could preach a beautiful sermon about this day. He would tell everyone how he'd seen the bowels of hell, where not one but several devils rule. But he would also speak of angels, man-angels who saw in his survival hope for their own.

One bullet landed, then another, then another, hammering the preacher's chest to the ground. The single lightbulb was fading.

"I bet you regret . . ." He heard the fat man's voice trail off as though it were moving farther and farther away from his ear.

Regrets? Did he have any? What would be the meaning of life, or death, without some lingering regrets?

Maybe he shouldn't have preached those "sermons to the beast," as he liked to think of them. But someone needed to stir the flock out of their stupor, the comfort that religion allowed them, that it was okay to have wretched lives here on earth so long as Heaven was glowing ahead. Maybe his death would do just that, move his people to revolt, to demand justice for themselves while requesting it for him. Or maybe his death would have no relevance at all. He would simply join a long list of martyrs and his name would vanish from his countrymen's lips as soon as his body was placed in the ground.

Oh, what a great sermon he could have preached about this, but alas he would never be able to. There would be no resurrection. He wouldn't sprout wings and soar to the clouds, vomit the bullets, whole, out of his mouth. The battle would be someone else's to fight from now on. And yet he had not been completely defeated. The wound on the fat man's face wasn't what he had hoped; he hadn't blinded him or removed some of his teeth, but at least he'd left a mark on him, a brand that he would carry for the rest of his life. Every time he looked in the mirror, he would have to confront this mark and remember him. Whenever people asked what happened to his face, he would have to tell a lie, a lie that would further remind him of the truth.

8

Anne had no idea where she was finding all this strength to run, but as she raced toward the barracks, she felt as though she were parting the night around her, creating a new path with every leap. She was speeding by everything so fast that it all became a dusky blur, all darks and grays, barely any shadows. She left Rue Tirremasse to join Rue du Peuple, the people's street, then Rue des Miracles, the street of miracles, and then Rue de l'Enterrement, burial street. She passed the archives building, the public school, Lycée Pétion, the old cathedral. As she neared Casernes, she charged through a pitiful pack of emaciated dogs fighting over scraps of garbage in the middle of the street. They joined her in her run for a while, then scattered and reunited, returning to the same refuse pile.

The streets were otherwise so empty that she felt she was the only person still alive in the entire city and that thought kept her running, and she would continue to run until something was able to stop her.

9

Rosalie rushed into the fat man's office, squatting in firing position. Behind her was a large cadre of military officers and militiamen, all with pistols and rifles drawn. The fat man was bent over his dead prisoner, checking for throbbing arteries in his neck. His face was covered with blood, and as he staggered to his feet he needed help from his colleagues to stand and lean against his desk.

"What have you done?" Rosalie shouted, her pistol aimed at his head.

"He attacked me," the fat man replied, catching his breath.

"How could you let this happen?" Rosalie slowly lowered her pistol. She seemed aware that all the wardens and militiamen were watching her and taking note of her reaction. She was like the queen of a fire ant nest. If she needed to, she could leave the other ants behind to attack, but she didn't. Not yet.

"I told you to let him go," she said.

When he looked down at the preacher's corpse, his arms and legs spread out, a puddle of blood growing around his torso, the fat man wanted to vomit. Since he'd disobeyed the palace's orders twice now, it was possible that he would be arrested, even executed.

He took a few steps away from the body. Stumbling past his colleagues, he tottered through the prison corridor, and soon he was out in the yard where the prisoners were allowed an hour in the sunlight each day.

"Where are you going?" Rosalie was following him.

He kept on walking until he'd crossed the entire yard, shuffling through a smaller building until he was outside again, this time in a patch of dried-out dandelion weeds near the front gates. It was only then that he emptied his stomach and once he'd begun, it seemed as if his retching would never stop.

At first he was alone out there near the gates; then Rosalie and the others joined him, circling him.

When there was nothing left in his stomach, Rosalie leaned toward him and said, "You're not well. I'll take you home."

"I'll get there myself," he said.

Then Rosalie signaled for the gatekeeper, whom the wardens had nicknamed Legba, to open the gates to let him out.

"You should be all right," Rosalie said, patting him on the back. "I'll think of something to explain all this."

He didn't feel reassured. Ultimately she would do what was best for her, taking responsibility if the president changed his mind once again and applauded the preacher's death or leaving the blame on him if she was reproached.

He walked out through the front gate thinking he was going to be shot in the back, either by his colleagues or by Legba, the gatekeeper. However, he managed to cross the threshold alive.

Once he was out on the street, he felt for his face, finding his fingertips delving inside his own flesh, as though he'd been wearing a rubber mask that was peeling away. Following the contour of the prison wall, he continued walking until he thought he was out of the range of fire, then stood at the corner on the edge of the block where the prison ended and the rest of the neighborhood began.

What would he do now? Where would he go? He should go to a hospital, but would he be safe there?

He felt another urge to retch, but even as his body tried its best to pour out his stomach contents, nothing came out. Then something hit him, something like a large, blind animal fleeing at a hundred miles per hour.

It was a woman, a madwoman it seemed. She was wearing a white satin nightgown that looked like a full slip. The nightgown was entirely soaked with sweat that glued it to her bony body. Her short hair was wild, as though each strand were standing up in protest, her eyes filled with rage and confusion.

After she'd slammed her body into his, she stopped and looked up at his lacerated face. He hoped she wasn't someone he'd harmed or nearly killed, someone who'd been in the torture chamber adjacent to his office, for he wanted sympathy, compassion from her. He wanted her to have pity on him, take him to her house and bandage him. Even if she despised him for some reason or another, he wanted her to help him, so he quickly mouthed the word "Tanpri," Please, and heard the same word come out of her mouth at the same time, and he remembered how his mother used to say that when you spoke the exact same words as someone else at the exact same time, it meant that the two of you would die on the same day. He hoped that his plea merging with hers wouldn't lead to her dying sooner than she was supposed to. Who was she, anyway? Was she a mother, a wife, a sister who was keeping a vigil for someone? Was she the one who called out "Jean" each time a new prisoner was brought in, the one in whose direction the officers and militiamen often shot?

He felt dizzy and, forgetting his own massive size and the fact that he could easily slam her down to the ground with his weight, he leaned toward her. She opened her arms and somehow managed to catch him and hold him upright. She was still looking closely at his face, her hands reaching over to touch his wounds in a way that seemed both healing and curious. She grabbed his head and sobbed in his hair.

"In there," she said. "I need to go in there."

"People who go in there," he said slowly, "don't come out."

At that moment he would have done anything to keep her with him. Besides, he wasn't lying. If she went in there, at that time of night, the men would make her all kinds of false promises, then have their way with her.

"Let's go," he said. "Quickly."

She looked at his face again, reached up and picked a few large splinters out of the wound, then followed him.

His home wasn't too far away. They walked fast, hurrying past the soccer stadium and the cemetery. Her body stiffened and she seemed to hold her breath until they passed the cemetery. He decided not to question her about that. Perhaps if she weren't a little mad, she wouldn't have been helping him at all.

10

When he got home, he stumbled onto the bare mattress on his bedroom floor and fell asleep. He didn't care whether or not he bled to death, didn't care about the cuts on his swelling face. He was happy she was there to watch him sleep or maybe even crawl up next to him and share his bed. In the morning, he would make all the important decisions that needed to be made, but for now all he wanted to do was slip into the kind of slumber from which it seemed there would be no awakening.

1 1

His face had stopped bleeding, but it was now covered with several layers of blood. She watched as the tint of the blood faded from bright red to dark brown to almost black.

The sun was coming up with a gentleness that surprised her. It was the reverse of what was happening to his face. First the black mist dulled to gray, then to the slight orange tint of a sunrise, then finally to the sheerness of glass.

From his louvered window, she watched an early-morning funeral procession on its way to the cemetery. There was no fanfare, no musical band accompanying the hearse and the family members walking behind it. Perhaps these people, who looked as though they were muffling their sobs with their dark handkerchiefs, were indigents who couldn't afford a more elaborate afternoon funeral and were so ashamed of this that they preferred to bury their loved one when most people were still asleep.

Once the funeral procession had passed, she looked

around his house for something to clean his even more enlarged face. The house was mostly empty save for the mattress he was lying on, a few pieces of clothing scattered here and there, some toiletries in the bathroom, and a few rusty forks and spoons in his kitchen. There was nothing with which to dress his wound. So she decided to go out and find a few pieces of ginger, a small bottle of honey, and some yerba buena with which to make an infusion for him.

On the street she did her best to avoid the cemetery. There were a few people out already, hurrying as if they were late for appointments made for the night before. She lowered her head as these people walked by her, staring.

There were only a few vendors in the open market when she arrived. The first one she approached, a skeletal dwarf with a large head, had a radio on, which was reporting some news from the night before. He had the ginger, yerba buena, and honey she needed, but she had no money to pay for anything. She didn't even have any clothes on, aside from her nightgown.

The vendor told her she could have these things if she would come back later and pay him. They weren't expensive, just five gourdes total, for everything.

"Are you buying these for a sick person?" he asked.

She nodded.

It occurred to her that maybe he was giving them to her because he thought she was a healer or a madwoman who all of a sudden was sobbing.

He was dreaming. Once again he was a boy in Léogâne, and he and his mother were working together in her garden. It was a cool morning and the sun was just rising, a golden mist surrounding them.

The earth was warm and moist when he touched it, the seedbeds smelling of decaying vegetable peel. As the sun rose higher in the sky, he could hear cocks crowing, dogs barking, birdcalls, and wings flapping, and his father gently moving toward his mother and himself to quietly watch them work before heading out to one of his early-morning mason lodge meetings.

Once more he was alone in the garden with his mother. Her long thick black hair, freed from the dark rag she usually kept it wrapped in, rose and fell on her shoulders in the morning breeze. Around them the seeds they'd planted together had magically taken root and were turning into trees—mango, papaya, guava, and avocado trees. From among the roots, herbs, and healing weeds, his mother reached down and plucked a bundled fern, a fèy wònt, a mimosa pudica or shame plant. She took one of his hands and guided it toward the tiny leaflets. When his index finger touched the prickly spine, the little leaves collapsed onto themselves as if to shut him out. She motioned for him to wait a while, for she never spoke in his dreams, and magically the leaves turned outward and reopened. She encouraged him to try this a few more times, tapping the shame plant to watch it close, then open and close once more. Then she handed him a sprig, motioning for him to hold on to it.

His dream abruptly ended with the sound of his front door being opened and shut. He sat up quickly to receive his visitor, reaching for his .38 where he usually kept it on the floor near the mattress by his head. But he didn't find it there. Emptied of bullets, it had remained, like his car and his hidden money, at the barracks. Then the events of the previous night came back to the forefront of his mind. The wait. The church. The minister. The shots. His throbbing, itching face, which felt as though it were being clawed. And this woman, this woman who had opened and closed his door, this woman who was standing there in a nightgown or a slip, covered with dirt and blood (his blood?), her eyes reddened, her face streaked with tears. This woman, she was holding a bottle of honey, three pieces of ginger, and a sprig of yerba buena that she probably meant to pound into some concoction to place on the wound on his face. This woman? Who was she again?

He was afraid to ask her name, afraid that he would recognize it. Maybe she was someone he'd been with before, someone he'd once brought home when he was too drunk to remember.

He was relieved when she asked a question first. And though she looked shell-shocked and insane, her voice didn't sound it. It was as calm as a stream or one of those tranquil brooks his mother was repeatedly taking him to in his dreams.

"What did they do to *you?*" she asked.

This was the most forgiving question he'd ever been asked. It suddenly opened a door, produced a small path, which he could follow.

"I'm free," he said. "I finally escaped."

Her posture was crooked, but her mind seemed clear. She had placed her wares on the floor, laid them out one by one at the foot of the mattress.

One day he would try to make her understand why he'd put it like that. In many ways it was true. He had escaped from his life. He could no longer return to it, no longer wanted to.

He would tell her the real truth later, much later, once he'd told her a series of other things, about his mother, his father, the garden, Léogâne.

What made him think there would be a later? Why was he so sure that she wasn't going to walk out on him in the next minute, the next hour, even the next day? Because she also looked as though there was something she was anxious to tell. Perhaps it was the thing that just then was making her cry. Or maybe it was the answer to those very questions that he so wanted to ask: Why had she been outside the prison so late at night? Who was *she* waiting for?

It was obvious that she now felt she'd been there to save him, to usher him back home and heal him.

1 3

It would be impossible to explain all that followed, to her daughter or to anyone. It wasn't that she thought the fat man was her half brother, the one who'd disappeared into the sea so long ago, that this girth, this vastness was something the youngest child in her family had garnered from his lost years of inhaling seawater and weeds. It wasn't that she thought he'd emerged from the cemetery, enlarged by the bones and souls of other ghosts. It wasn't that she believed he could help her find her stepbrother, the minister, the one they'd just arrested and taken to jail the night before. It wasn't that she was thinking of the self-sacrificing martyrs who now made miracles possible: Saint Rose de Lima, who'd sanded and blistered her face with peppers to avoid vanity; Saint Veronica, who wiped floors with her tongue; or Saint Solange, who, after being decapitated, had carried her own head to a church altar. It wasn't even that it had occurred to her that if he wasn't one of her brothers he was surely someone else's, who had just surfaced from another kind of grave. Maybe it was none of these things. Maybe it was all of them. Plus a hollow grief extended over all these years, a penance procession that has yet to end.

A few minutes later, when he got his landlord, the doctor, out of bed to sew his face, she watched from a corner as the doctor pulled a silver thread in and out of his skin. It seemed like some kind of torture, the type you might inflict on someone you truly hated, but he didn't seem very pained from it. Heeding the doctor's warning that if he grimaced too much or insisted on smoking a cigarette while his wound was being sewed, his face would heal in a way that would make him look like a monster, he remained still until the doctor was done.

She couldn't easily remember when she'd first heard that her stepbrother, the preacher, had died. It might have been from the vendor's radio, the one that was giving the news that morning. Or it may have been from the doctor's casual chatter, something about "a preacher from Bel-Air killing himself at Casernes." But she'd slipped out of her own body then, just as now.

When her daughter called her from Lakeland after her husband's confession to ask, "Manman, how do you love him?" she was sitting at the kitchen table, eating a piece of pie. It was not what she thought she'd be doing when that question finally came. Like her husband, she'd thought she might be on a trip, some kind of journey with her daughter. She had imagined the two of them, just the girls, on the ocean, on a cruise liner or some other place from which her daughter couldn't escape. But here they are, thousands of miles apart and not even looking into each other's eyes as she attempts an explanation.

"He tell you?" Instead she replies with another question.

"Yes," the daughter says. Her voice is cold and dry, unlike the high-pitched shrill it was when she'd been so worried about her father's disappearance earlier. From the tone of her daughter's voice, she gathers that their child is already passing judgment on them. And she hasn't even heard the whole story.

She puts her spoon down next to her half-eaten piece of pie, walks over to the garbage pail, and drops it in. Now she's tapping her fingers against the telephone mouthpiece and clicking her tongue, to eliminate the distracting silence all around her.

"Is there more?" the daughter says. And she sounds afraid that the "more," the rest, the whole story could be worse than what she's already heard.

Unlike her husband, she would never know how to tell a story like this, how to decipher all the details and make sense of them. But this much she wants her daughter to know.

"What he told you, he want to tell you for long time," she hears herself whispering now in her awful English. But in her head, her words have a little more order. It was a miracle, be it a sad one. The day after she met her daughter's father, he used most of the money he was keeping in his mattress to procure them passage on a Pan American flight to New York. And he had never killed anyone again.

When they arrived in New York and an old army friend of his met them at the airport and he introduced her as his wife, she did not disagree. Theirs became a kind of benevolent collaboration, a conspirational friendship. With few others to turn to, it became love. Yes, love. But not the kind of love her daughter or girls like her stumbled into or might expect one day. It was a more strained kind of attachment, yet she could no longer imagine her life without it.

In the early years, there had been more silence than words between them. But when their daughter was born, they were forced to talk to and about her. And when their daughter began to talk back, it made things all that much easier. She was like an orator at a pantomime. She was their Ka, their good angel.

After her daughter was born, she and her husband would talk about her brother. But only briefly. He referring to his "last prisoner," the one that scarred his face, and she to "my stepbrother, the famous preacher," neither of them venturing beyond these coded utterances, dreading the day when someone other than themselves would more fully convene the two halves of this same person.

He endorsed the public story, the one that the preacher had killed himself. And she accepted that he had only arrested him and turned him over to someone else. Neither believing the other nor themselves. But never delving too far back in time, beyond the night they met. She never saw any of the articles that were eventually written about her brother's death. She was too busy concentrating on and revising who she was now, or who she wanted to become.

In the middle of all this incoherent muttering, she realized that her daughter had hung up the phone. Or maybe the phone had come out of the wall while she was pacing back and forth across the kitchen floor. There was now a strange mechanical voice on the line telling her to "hang up and try again."

She wished she had someone with her now, to get her past the silence that would follow the trying again. She was no longer used to this particular type of loneliness, this feeling that you could be alive or dead and no one would know. She had hoped to close the call by saying something tender and affectionate to her daughter, something like, "You are mine and I love you." Or maybe she would reach for a now useless cliché, one that she had been reciting to herself all these years, that atonement, reparation, was possible and available for everyone. Or maybe she would think of some unrelated anecdote, a parable, another miracle story, or even some pleasantry, a joke. Anything to keep them both talking. But her daughter was already gone, lost, accidentally or purposely, in the hum of the dial tone.

There was no way to escape this dread anymore, this pendulum between regret and forgiveness, this fright that the most important relationships of her life were always on the verge of being severed or lost, that the people closest to her were always disappearing. The spirits had long since stopped coming through her body via her mysterious spells, which she now knew had a longish name with a series of nearly redundant syllables. These spirits, they'd left her for good the morning that the news was broadcast on the radio that her brother had set his body on fire in the prison yard at dawn, leaving behind no corpse to bury, no trace of himself at all.

ACKNOWLEDGMENTS

For my father, who, thank goodness, is not in this book. And for my cousin Hans Adonis, who is the book's parènn, because of all the Duvalier-era research he so lovingly bombarded me with.

Thank you, Laura Hruska, Charles Rowell, Jacqueline Johnson, Brad Morrow, Deborah Treisman, Alice Quinn, Leslie Casimir, Nicole Aragi, and Robin Desser for midwifing and support.

In "The Dew Breaker," the line "Impossible to deepen that night" is from Graham Greene's novel about Haiti, *The Comedians*. "Tu deviens un véritable gendarme, un bourreau" is from Jacques Stephen Alexis' *Compère Soleil General*. I'm grateful to Patrick Lemoine for his extremely powerful memoir, *Fort Dimanche, Dungeon of Death*. And to Bernard Diederich and Al Burt for their wonderful book *Papa Doc and the Tonton Macoutes*.

And in one great big breath, welcome to our brood,

Zora dear, we love you so much. Manman Nick, Tonton Moïse, you're greatly missed. We row on without you, but I know we'll meet again.

And finally—

Question:

Two trees, 10 feet apart. Taller tree, 50 feet tall, casts a 20-foot shadow. Shorter tree casts a 15-foot shadow. The sun's shining on each tree from the same angle. How tall is the shorter tree?

Answer:

$$\frac{\text{height of big tree (50)}}{\text{length of shadow (20)}} = \frac{\text{height of small tree (x)}}{\text{length of shadow (15)}}$$

$$\frac{50 = x}{20 = 15}$$

$$\frac{20x = 750}{20}$$

The shorter tree (x) is 37.5 feet tall.

Question and answer courtesy of *Master the GED* (2003 edition), published by Thompson/Arco, written by Ronald Kaprov, Steffi Kaprov, and Barbara Hull.